Postmodern Blues

Victor Cabas

Hypocrite Press
Charlottesville, VA
http://www.hypocritepress.org

Introduction

Better Late Than Never

by Caine O'Rear

I spoke with Victor Cabas about *Postmodern Blues* in early 2018, just a few weeks before he died unexpectedly of a heart attack at the age of 69. Over Christmas break that year I'd found some of the early chapters he'd given me nearly a decade prior. As I re-read them that winter I found myself still riveted by the story, still laughing out loud, and finally, left wanting more.

"We've got to get moving on this thing and get it published," I told him over the phone. "It's too good not to be read." Victor was a great believer in Time, and he moved at his own pace. I felt he needed a kick in the groin.

He seemed excited by my renewed interest, adding that it was basically done and that he'd read over it the past year and still liked it. "I'll have my secretary send you the rest of it," he said.

I was working as an editor in magazine publishing at the time, and suggested trying to get an excerpt published somewhere. He seemed open to the idea, but he forgot to send it. Then one day in late February I got a text from a friend telling me he was gone.

*****

Cabas began writing *Postmodern Blues* sometime in the 1990s, working on it off and on through the following decades with periodic bursts of sustained effort. Then he would leave it alone, for years even, perhaps for nearly a decade in one case. I stopped inquiring about the book during our phone conversations, as I could tell it nagged him that it wasn't finished. But he was a man of many pursuits. Between teaching, working his cattle farm, playing weekly music gigs, and buying, selling and repairing vintage guitars — lots of them — there wasn't always time to put pen to paper.

In the summer of 2008 he took a break from teaching summer school at the University of Virginia, and in a burst of output, much of the book was written. I remember him being giddy the day he handed me those first chapters. "It's gonna be good," he beamed with a Mephisthophelian grin, before pausing. "Well ... at least it'll be funny."

1

The novel tells the story of Jack Shock, an English professor who, as the novel opens, is drinking himself to near death in the highlands of Guatemala (where Cabas, in his words, "once got stoned in the biblical sense" by a horde of rock-wielding Mayans in a case of mistaken identity). The rest of the story unfolds in Washington, D.C. and the classrooms and downtown bars of Charlottesville. The main character, and much of the story, cribs from Cabas's own life, but the two are far from carbon copies of one another.

Postmodern Blues is a book of many hats. On one level, it details a man's struggle with alcoholism in almost Dostoevskian fashion; the novel's cast of barflies and ne'er do wells leap off the page in vivid Technicolor and bear the blemished edges of a humanity not yet incised by the self-correction of digital culture. It is also a picaresque romp in the tradition of Henry Fielding's *Tom Jones*, one of Cabas's favorite books and one that Shock quotes from more than once — "Hide, and if they find you, lie." For Jack Shock, "they" are the Bernard Vandillinghams, Charlie Bledsoes and Jackson Prileaus of the world.

Thomas Wolfe once observed that all fiction is largely autobiographical. As such, it is no surprise that the character of Shock shares some qualities with the author, but for those who knew him, it's obvious it's not a facsimile of the man. The sections in the book that satirize academia recall Kingsley Amis' *Lucky Jim*, a work Cabas himself taught in "The Jim Class," along with Joseph Conrad's *Lord Jim* and *Huckleberry Finn*. (Cabas, who quit drinking in his early 40s, once quipped that "Only an alcoholic would teach a class called 'The Jim Class.'")

The novel's apocalyptic pull recalls Joseph Conrad as well as Malcolm Lowry's *Under The Volcano*, another tale of rot and exile in Paradise by way of demon rum. But perhaps more than anything else, *Postmodern Blues* is a love story, shot through with every beautiful and problematic complication our capacity for loving (and loathing) creates.

As for Shock, Cabas said he based him in part on a professor he had while earning his Phd in upstate New York. The professor was a Texan of the Rabelaisian sort who dedicated his book on Conrad's "metaphysics of darkness" to Larry, Moe and Curly -- a signature Shock adopts himself. Cabas told me a story years ago about how one afternoon the two were walking to a bar, seeking sanctuary from the brutality of a Buffalo winter, when they passed a strip club that had the portraits of the performers framed in the window, like you sometimes see on Bourbon Street. "She looks pretty good for a stripper," Cabas remarked offhandedly. "I know," his mentor deadpanned, "I was married to her."

Throughout his professional life, Cabas remained suspicious of academics. Like Shock, he abhorred the cynicism of the postmodern ethic, and the idea that the critic is paramount. As Shock tells of his former student Susan Monteith:

> *I didn't want to sound like a college professor, not to her, not that I was much of one. Like Susan Monteith, I had pretty much had my fill of academic life. But I didn't feel like copping an attitude. Academia was no phonier than any other form of corporate self-aggrandizement. It hadn't always been the moral equivalent of Exxon and somewhere at someplace small it was probably still mostly about teaching. But while I'd been at the University it had almost always had the stink of snake oil.*

I first met Cabas as a student at the University of Virginia, when I took his "Mississippi In Song And Story" class, which mostly concerned the novels of William Faulkner and lyrics of bluesman Robert Johnson. He walked into the classroom at Bryan Hall the first day of class wearing dark sunglasses, a straw hat, torn jeans with a star patch over one knee, and Jesus sandals. As he was walking in, he started addressing the class. "If I had taken this class at your age," he said, "I would've dropped it in a New York minute, because you are going to work. I went to summer school at the University of Hawaii, and let me tell you, it ain't exactly an intellectual powerhouse." He seemed more Douglas MacArthur than Jerry Garcia, despite the appearance. It turned out to be the best — and most challenging — course I took at UVA. I've heard others say the same.

"The saying is, those who can't do, teach — but it's a noble profession," he once said wryly. His students well recall such banter — and how he took teaching seriously. But it always bothered him when professors talked down their students and his humor was an honest balance. He felt that books had transformative power and could change lives, and he seemed to genuinely care for each of them. "Dr. Cabas never had children but often thought of the many students he worked with at the College as his sons," wrote Kenneth Townsend, a friend and economics professor at Hampden-Sydney, shortly after his passing.

Much like Shock's, Cabas' father was an Air Force Brigadier General and renowned war pilot named Victor N. Cabas, who passed away at the age of 98, just six months after his son died. The elder Cabas flew more than 300 missions in World War II before flying combat missions in Korea and Vietnam and was said to have seen more aerial warfare than any man on earth. Born in Newport News, Virginia, the younger Cabas spent much of his youth in South Carolina, where he attended high school and was something of a military brat as a kid, living in England and Hawaii for a spell.

It was at UVA where Cabas encountered Herman Melville's *Moby-Dick* for the first time, and the book made such an impression that it inspired him to become an academic. He was accepted to the University of Virginia School of

Law, but after sitting in on classes as an undergraduate, he decided it was like "reading your car manual over and over again." Instead of pursuing law he accepted a scholarship at State University of New York at Buffalo where he wrote his dissertation on the use of meta-drama in Shakespeare's plays and earned his doctorate in literature in 1974.

In the mid-70s he began his academic teaching career in the English Department at the University of Virginia. He did not put himself up for tenure and started teaching at Hampden-Sydney shortly thereafter in the Rhetoric Department, where in addition to writing, he taught Shakespeare, Melville, Faulkner, the Civil War, American Blues Music, and Cormac McCarthy's *Blood Meridian*, as well as other subjects.

However, it was actually music that was Cabas' foremost love in life, especially the blues of the Mississippi Delta, and in particular the songs and guitar playing of Robert Johnson. Those sentiments are echoed by Shock:

> *I remember the first time I heard that voice [of Johnson's]. I was at a party, and I had just taken a hit of reefer. The song was 'Kind Hearted Woman' ... The counterpoint of voice and guitar, both distorting sound, the voice like a record slowing down, and the triplet A chord on the seventh fret . . . And then soaring above it came that eerie falsetto 'Oo, baby, my life won't be the same,' the sound rising above the forlorn desire of the words themselves.*

Cabas was never happier than when he was playing guitar, whether on one of his beloved arch-tops or some obscure electric belted through a vintage tube amp. He knew a great deal about American roots music and as a guitarist he was a respected bottleneck slide player, with a raw, feral style that befitted his personality. According to Townsend, Eric Clapton once called Cabas' house and asked if he'd be playing a party the Brit was attending in the area. Vic responded, "Eric who?"

In the book, Shock repeatedly filters the events of his life through the prism of old blues lyrics from masters like Johnson, Son House, Bukka White, and Blind Lemon Jefferson. Still, the curiousness of this tendency is not lost on him as a Southern white male:

> *Why did I identify with a black man whose world I could know only in books and records? Maybe it was the car wreck that orphaned me as completely as if my father had died in it too. Or the sick in me that attracted me to a woman like Donna Gordon Prileau.*

I heard many stories over the years from Cabas' bacchanalian, post-divorce drinking days, a time that he recalled fondly. A large section of the book transpires in the bars of Charlottesville's downtown mall. Back then, Charlottesville's downtown scene was an orbit of artists, writers and scholarly inebriates. The playwright and actor Sam Shepard lived nearby, raising horses, and could often be found slaking his thirst at Miller's, a former drugstore turned bar. Cabas was regarded as a man to know in bohemian circles, frequently sought out for mentoring from aspiring artists and musicians. "Charlottesville bartenders. All of them had college degrees. About half of them were English majors," Shock muses. This was when Charlottesville was still a laid-back Southern college town, quite different from the hedge-fund village and showpiece it would become. Dave Matthews had just started performing in public and would give Cabas his early demos for feedback. Matthews even played the role of a drunken fratboy in a play Cabas wrote that was performed at the local playhouse Live Arts. Shock, it seems, might have known him too:

> *Sonnybuck and I walked along the bar, past the musician strumming an old Ovation guitar. It was a guy named Dave who had worked there two years ago when he had a Mr. T haircut. Eyes half-closed, he was singing 'All Along the Watchtower,' as if everything in his world depended on it.*

Even after he quit drinking, Cabas continued to perform on Charlottesville's Downtown Mall through the late '90s, setting up on the street, sometimes solo, sometimes with a small band, and playing for tips. He played and sang through an amp, so you could hear that unmistakable bellow from the other side of the mall. But someone eventually complained, as people are wont to do, saying he was violating the noise ordinance, and that was that. Understandably, the old townie was ticked; he loved playing there, seeing his friends and a cavalcade of former students among the crowd.

As I think back on these elements that were part of Cabas's world I am reminded of something the novelist James Salter once said: "there comes a time in life, when you realize that everything is a dream; only those things which are written down have any possibility of being real." For everyone who knew Victor, and his fans were numerous, we're lucky to have this record from the man. It is not a portrait of his life, but in a way, it does feel real, as real as a visit with an old friend, one who now lives in that undiscovered country from which no traveler returns.

Postmodern Blues

1. Death Letter

I got a letter this morning.
How do you reckon that it read?

Son House

When we got to the top of the rise she hit the brakes hard. The car rocked twice on its bad shocks and stopped.

"Get out!" she said.

I looked at her. She had the good, tight body of a Golden Gloves bantam-weight and, too bad for her, a face to go with it. Someone else had given her that broken nose and with it a look of one of Gauguin's Tahitian princesses. But there had been moments during the two weeks I'd lived with her when if it hadn't been against my principles, I'd have loved to take a poke at her.

"Get out!" she said again. I got out. All I owned was in the General's B-4 bag. I was lucky to get it before she floored the gas pedal. She must have planned to stop where she had because it was the only place on the mountain road where you could turn around in that big motorboat-sized car she drove, some kind of Dodge from the seventies with a big block engine that was hell on gas. When she got the car turned around she laid a long twisting snake of rubber fishtailing.

At least she'd left me with a view. The mountain was scrub, but down below I could see the deep blue waters of Lago Atitlán. The two big volcanoes off to the right, named for saints — I forget their names— were like Madonna's breast prongs, sharp perfect cones. On the shore across from the mountains, I could see the towns of Panachel and Jucanaya. The lake looked, as Henry T. had said of another one, like the earth's eye. It was hard to feel sorry for yourself looking at a view like that. So I sat down and lit up my last hit of reefer and looked it over. It was about eleven o'clock, a couple of hours before the wind called the Chocomil would come up and turn the mirror-smooth waters of the lake into a cauldron. The wind that washes away sins the Mayans called it. I had the feeling I was going to need a Chocomil of my own before long. There was seven miles of bad road waiting for me back home. But first I had to get home. Home. What home I asked. I thought for a moment of the cabin in the mountains that no doubt my ex-wife had sold by now. Then I thought of the house in Washington where my father, so the letter said, was on his way out.

I was still sitting there a half hour later when the cavalry arrived: John Rhodes driving up in his Deux Chevaux, the kind of luck I almost never have. Except for Katie and Marco, he was the only person in Guatemala I knew who owned a car. He slowed up and rolled his window down.

"Jack," he said, "someone told me you had to catch a plane."

"Yeah. I do."

I got in. The someone would have to have been Marco. We'd stayed up late the night before at his bar The Last Resort drinking Gallianos. Marco had made his pile working on the Alaska pipeline, driving up every year for five months of summer labor. After six years of that he'd come back home to Chi-Chi Tenengo, high in the mountains where the Quetzals lived, what few were left. By then Chi-Chi was a place the government troops killed you for being from, so Marco bought a bar in Pana. It was a good place to drink, eat, pick up a girl, smoke a little reefer. All they ever played there were Talking Heads songs, which, though I'd never much liked them back home, I grew steadily fond of until I'd heard them so much that with just the hint of a phrase from "Psycho Killer" I had a physical reaction of loathing. Probably it had something to do with my profession. A talking head after all was a pretty good description of a college professor, although bullshit monster sometimes seemed nearer the mark.

"I saw Katie on the road." John was looking at me, as if he was trying to fathom what must have happened between us.

"Moving pretty fast?"

"Very fast."

"Hell of a woman," I said.

I'd gotten to know John a couple of months earlier at a party. John Rhodes was tall, broad-shouldered, with a tapering waist, generous grey eyes and a smile. In the seventies he'd drifted south from L.A., living in Baha, California, Puerto Vallarta, and then in Livingston on the gulf coast of Gautemala, where he surfed and loafed and maybe even invited his soul. He didn't want to go home, but he was broke and he'd gotten the idea of importing satellite dishes to Guatemala for the suburban fat cats and hotels in Guat City. Now he was rich by Guatemalan standards and better yet, indispensable. In a country where they killed you for straying down the wrong road, or laughing at the wrong line, indispensable was better than rich.

Sixteen years before he'd fallen in love with beautiful Concha, a general's daughter, though she'd run to fat a little. Concha still had her looks. She fortified herself against the crows' feet and love handles of middle age with cocaine and Quaaludes and a string of interchangeable partners. Briefly I'd been one of them. When he picked me up, John Rhodes was returning to the city after visiting the daughter he'd fathered in that dead-letter affair fourteen years ago.

"How's Camilla?" I asked.

"She's good," he said.

John wanted to get her to school in the States and I'd agreed to help him find one. She seemed not only to have survived her mother's life but to be untouched by it.

"I heard about your father from Marco," John said, glancing at me. "Is it bad?"

"It must be," I said.

Dying, Sam had written. For a while we rode on in silence. The country we were driving through was steep rolling hills covered in green stubble. There were no trees and no pastures; the Indians cut the wood for fires as fast as it grew. They kept no pigs or cows, just chickens and the odd horse you'd see tethered along the roadside. The Pan American, broken and potholed as a Virginia back road, was almost bare of traffic, though it was the biggest highway in all the country. We passed two Indian men riding bareback on an old white horse. They were wearing white straw hats and faded rebozos of lilac and blue, and as always they were smiling. The Mayans smiled even when I greeted them with the only word I knew of their tongue: Nahumpoc, which means "No money." From the first I'd loved the look of these people: their faces delicate, their limbs shapely, their children shy and sweet, smiling when a stranger greeted them in passing. They lived on nothing, or next to it — a few dollars a day would feed a family — and the children worked from a very early age.

"When does your plane leave?" John asked, breaking into my thoughts.

"Tomorrow," I said.

"Where will you be staying?"

"I thought I'd sleep in the airport."

"You can't do that," he said. "They close it at midnight"

He looked at me.

"Do you have money?"

I told him all I had was a ticket home and eight quetzals — about five dollars.

"You'll need more than that to get out of the country." He laughed, shaking his head. "There's a tax you've got to pay to leave. Forty Quetzals."

The way my luck had been running lately, none of this exactly surprised me. Here I was again, shipwrecked, this time in the boonies of Central America. Not that there was anyone to blame for it but me, Jack Shock, chief architect of my misfortunes.

"Shit," I said.

John Rhodes laughed.

"We'll think of something," he said.

It was John Rhodes who lent me the money to pay the departure tax, gave me one of the two rooms the management reserved for him at the Biltmore to keep the television screens filled with what seemed like an endless program of soap operas and talk shows in Spanish, and Latin Rod Stewart and Tina Turner impersonators. He gave me money for a good Italian dinner and told me where to find it. He told me where to find the American bars and even advice about where to get safely laid. Company of any sort didn't seem an urgent need right at the moment. But after a month of eating Katie's tortillas, the manicotti dinner was sure welcome.

About ten o'clock an Indian woman knocked discreetly and entered with a little tray of Godiva chocolates and a glass of Dubonnet and gave me a rubdown that left me feeling like I'd had a hit of good reefer. The next morning John got me up and took me to the airport. He was the kind of man you wish you could bottle up and spread around, or at least take with you. But when I shook his hand good-bye I knew I probably wouldn't see him again for a long, long time, if ever.

"I owe you," I said.

"Stay away from wildcats, Jack," he said, winking.

I just grinned.

On the plane I could feel myself drifting off to sleep. I pulled out my wallet and shook out the two letters folded into squares the size of sugar packets. I unfolded one of them: It turned out to be the letter from Vandillingham, who as luck would have it, was serving as Chair that semester. Like the man who had written it, the letter was nasty, pointed and short.

Dear Shock,

Dean Webley informs me that unless you return to your teaching duties next semester you will be in default of contract and liable to dismissal. I have already directed that you be assigned a regular teaching load consisting of the undergraduate survey in Twentieth Century American Prose and a graduate seminar in Southern Narrative. Since your departure, neither course has been offered. While I have no sense that you have been personally missed, the Department is obligated to offer the courses you teach. It is with considerable pleasure that I forward this ultimatum: If you are not here by January 14, 1993, you will no longer be a member of the faculty of this university.

Very truly yours,

Bernard Vandillingham

Professor of English

    January 14th was ten days away. It was pleasant to think of the look I would see on old Bernie's face when I walked into his office on the morning of the 14th. Vandillingham wrote about and even looked like Alexander Pope, especially if you could have shrunk him and stuck a hump between his shoulder blades. He had the smile of a lamprey, one of those blood sucking eels they say Pope had died of eating.

    The other square unfolded more quickly. This was the letter that fetched me home. It was from Sam about the old man to whom I'd neither spoken nor written a word nor heard nor read one from him in two years.

Jack,

    Come quick. The General is dying.

    Love,

    Sam

2. Fixing to Die

I don't mind dying
Just hate to leave my children crying.
Bukka White

Late at night Dulles is a lonely place to fly into, especially in January with a couple of inches of frozen slush on the ground. The main terminal rises out of a concrete lake like a set from a *Star Trek* episode. Night turns the window walls glossy black as obsidian. I caught a glimpse of my reflection framed in tar and winced. I looked burnt down and beat to the wide, a refugee from the Manson cult. All I had to wear were dirty jeans and a Last Resort T-shirt I'd gotten from Marco. Two taxis turned me down before one agreed to take me to Capitol Hill. The driver, whom I privately dubbed Igor Mohammed because I wasn't sure which ethnicity went with his Eastern Mediterranean looks, grunted in answer to all my questions. I gave up finally; silence seemed more companionable than pig talk. The heater didn't heat, and I started to shiver so hard my teeth were knocking. It was a long, cold ride to the city, punctuated by bleak scenes of scarecrow tree stubble, alternating with views of concrete retaining walls. I felt like Bartleby looking out at Wall Street in one of his reveries. I too preferred not to. Then one of those damned Talking Heads songs started beating a tattoo in my skull; I tried to get a rhythm going with my chattering teeth and gave it up.

My career as an academic talking head had been in cold storage for the last two years while I had taken a so-called sabbatical to celebrate and mourn being tenured and divorced, although which was more to be celebrated and which mourned I wasn't sure. Robert Johnson, who couldn't make his own fortune, had made mine. The book I'd written on the place of his songs in the Southern literary tradition had managed to find an audience. First there were favorable reviews in some trendy academic journals. Then *The New Yorker* and the *New York Times Book Review* had praised the book as "readable" and "accessible." Not exactly virtues in academia these days but more or less what I'd aimed at. It had even made me a little money. A year later at the tenure witch trial, I was one of the accused in the annual procession to the scaffold. Would I go up in smoke? Would I find sanctuary as a colleague? The English Department hemmed and hawed over my case, its reigning Olympians being a crew of post modernists with little love for my subject. Vandillingham himself was the local duke of Foucault. What saved me, I think, was that during that month I was invited to New Haven to give a talk on the Faulkner chapter "Joe Christmas: A Hell Hound on his Trail." I was told that my talk made a useful

12

impression on one of the greats at Yale and that in turn won over the department, bar the Vandillingham faction, which after much furor, caved in.

It had been a close run thing, but Jack Shock had made it down the pipe. Although we hadn't lived together for some time, Donna had formally bailed out of our marriage during the nip and tuck phase of deliberations. She was pretty bitter about my success. She'd taken to sleeping with my best friend and chief rival for tenure, Bill Smalls, the shoo-in from Harvard, and that year's post modernist great white hope. His book *Shakespeare by Lacan* was nihilistic, opaque and very clever. Bill himself claimed that he had out Vandillinghamed Vandillingham. But in the end Robert Johnson, luckless and demon-haunted, had done for me what Lacan couldn't do for Bill. The department had hung, drawn and quartered him, and given me an office with a window.

I had lost my home, my wife, my best friend and in return I had a job in perpetuity impersonating a college professor in the company of men and women who wrote and talked in dead earnest about ideas that were to me a parody of thought about a parody of life.

I decided to make a run for it. As far as I knew, I wasn't coming back. My sabbatical led me to the Lesser Antilles. I sold my car and bought an old Cal 20, which three months later I hung on a reef in a storm off Bequay in the Grenadines. I sold the boat for salvage and took the money to Belize where I met a girl and then moved on. It went on like that for a while. I'd gotten a second year of unpaid leave by claiming more or less disingenuously to be working on a book on Márquez. What I was working on was learning Spanish from a Costa Rican surfer girl. That hadn't worked out either. All that I'd found in my travels had been a little bit of oblivion. Different countries, different situations, and now and again different women, Katie from Panachel being the last and not the least. In almost two years I had met no one that I knew from the States. The only person I'd even written to, other than the letter requesting leave, had been Sam.

Igor Mohamed drove us across the Memorial Bridge into the city and turned up Independence Avenue. We drove by some of the bars I'd been sloshed in underage, overage, and in between. The Tune Inn, with its wall of stuffed animal heads and blue-collar clientele, had been my favorite. In the eighties, like everything, it had been yuppified.

"Turn here," I said. We turned down the General's street and drove by Moynihan's house with its wall of plates painted by Picasso and residence of the General's least favorite senator. "That's the one," I said, pointing to a Georgian house with a rock facade. I could tell that Igor Mohammed, God bless his cynical heart, couldn't believe that someone who looked like me would be welcome, let alone reside in that house. Welcome, I'd never felt that. Live there, I had for more years than I had anyplace else.

It took a long time for my knocking on the door to get answered and I stood there shivering in my t-shirt and ragged jeans under Igor Mohammed's doubtful but proprietary gaze. He needn't have worried. I had no place to run to now but this one. Finally, the outside light flickered on and slowly the door opened. It was Sam.

"Jack," she said. "Oh, Jack! You're here! You're here!"

She took me into her arms and hugged me the way people hug prodigal sons in the scenic moments of thirties movies. Sam was the kind of girl Capra would have matched with Gary Cooper or Jimmy Stewart. Straight up, not hung up. A face lit by a light within. To me she had always been Cousin Sam, although she was no blood kin. Aunt Grace, my father's dead brother's wife, long dead herself, to me, had born her ten months after Uncle Mike had died.

"I'm Stoney, Sam," I said looking at her. She got her purse and paid off Igor Mohammed, who, charmed by Sam's neon smile and big tip, brought my bag to the door before he drove off.

We stood there a moment looking each other over. She was tall for a woman, maybe as tall as I. Her long hair, about as black as a crow's wing, and her eyes as blue as the waters of Atitlán. Not a great one for powder and paint. I was glad to see she still had a dusting of freckles across her nose and also still glad she had a way of smiling whenever I looked at her.

"You're so thin," she said.

"I'm all right."

"Your beard looks like a blackberry bramble."

She took my hand, hers so white and mine so dark that I seemed altogether from a different race.

"Is that really your skin, Jack?"

"It's me. You get a lot of sun down south." She smiled at my feeble wit.

"It's been two years, Jack." Then she hugged me again. She was crying now and I quit trying not to hug her back.

"I missed you!"

"Missed you too," I said.

We stood there awhile rocking, entwined. There was a long stretch of muffled sobs and whispers. Her hair smelled old-fashioned, like lilacs. Her face was buried in my chest and it felt wet like a warm rain. Then I started to feel something else holding her and gently pushed her from me and looked her in the eye.

"What's wrong with the old man?"

"It's cancer, Jack."

A cold stone dropped through my guts.

"What kind?"

"Liver"

"Oh no."

"It's metastasized"

"No. How long?"

"About three months."

"To live?"

"No, that's how long we've — I've known. He's dying."

"How long?" I asked again

"Any time." She was crying. "He could go any time." Then she added, "He's suffering. I think he's hung on to see you."

I couldn't think of anything to say. I could see the portrait of him at the foot of the staircase where it faced one of my mother. It had been painted in Bavaria in the forties just after they were married and before I was born. A major then, he was dressed in olive drab with a yellow and red eighth army patch on his shoulder. Before the surrender, the artist had made his living painting Nazi officers and the Third Reich's petty bureaucrats and out of habit he had teutonized the old man's face, arching the nose, lightening the hair. But he'd certainly caught my father's characteristic look. The fearless eyes of a peregrine. Something hooded and ruthless that you saw even when he sat at the head of the table carving the Sunday beef. Facing him was my mother, a plump, high-colored Dutch girl with laughing green eyes, and a full mouth. It had been many years since I'd seen her face in life; I'd never really gotten over her death. Neither had my father. He'd drunk the pain to sleep every night with blended Scotch whiskey, and sunk every year into an isolation that only Sam could draw him out from. I noticed that Sam was looking at the portrait too.

"Do you think it looks like him?"

"To the life," I said.

"And your Mom?"

"Not so much."

"I barely remember my mom at all."

"I know," I said.

Once again she came into my arms. I felt her against me all along my body. This is just what I don't need, I was thinking, Christ, it's almost incest. Again, I pushed her away as softly as I could.

"Where is he?" I asked.

"Upstairs, asleep."

"Shouldn't he be in a hospital?"

"He came home from Walter Reed last week. They say there's nothing they can do for him. And he wants to die at home."

"Does he get something for the pain?"

"Yes," she said, "I give him that."

"Will he know me?"

"Yes." She waited. "He's been asking for you, Jack."

I nodded. I felt empty of anything. I didn't even want a drink. I realized suddenly that the twelve hours I'd spent since I'd gotten on the plane in Guatemala City were the longest I'd gone without a drink or a cigarette since the boat wreck fifteen months before. But I was alive, at least. And here.

"Let's go up," I said.

We walked up the sweep of the curved staircase to the second floor bedrooms.

"He's in your room," she said.

"My room?"

"He wanted to stay there, Jack"

"Why? — because it's quiet?"

"I think he misses you, Jack."

I thought about that. I had too long a knowledge of the old man lying in there to credit her sentimental reading of his motives. My estrangement from him was visceral. I'd never known his praise. Moral support wasn't his long suit either. His comment when I told him that Donna had moved out was typical: "What are you going to do, Jack? Fall on your sword?"

We stood at the door to my bedroom. I looked at Sam but she shook her head and stepped back. Slowly I pushed the door open and went in. I heard the door pulled shut behind me. A small brass lamp on the night stand lighted his face. For a while I listened to the rhythm of his breathing. I drew closer. I couldn't remember ever looking at my father sleeping. I know I must have, maybe when I was a boy. Almost before I knew it I'd reached my hand to his face and touched his cheek with the back of my fingers. He stirred but didn't wake. Even in the dim light I could see the lines of his face. It made me think of a landscape glimpsed from a plane window over Arizona. The bones of his cheek and jaw were stretching the skin, the skull pushing through, foreshadowing. His face was inscrutable even in the last ravages of embattled mortality. There was a Windsor chair; I sat beside him, my hand on the bed next to his head, all kinds of things going through my mind, some crazy, some sad. After a while I must have slept because there was light at the window,

16

whether dawn or false dawn, I didn't know. I looked down at my father's face and almost as if I'd willed it, his eyes opened.

"Jack," he said. "Sam. Sam. Sam is —" He tried to finish but the pain froze him in mid-sentence.

"Dad," I said. That was all. I took his hand. Then slowly, as if he were drifting off to sleep, it went slack. My mind was empty of anything except a line from "Hellhound on my Trail": "Got to keep moving, got to keep moving, blues falling down like hail." Maybe there was a knack to living. Keep moving was about all I'd learned.

Time passed. I didn't sleep again.

I was looking past my father at the brown and blue incandescence of the dawn and I remembered suddenly a story his brother had told me of the last time they had seen their mother's face. She was running away with a man who rented a room from my grandfather. Her daughters, my father's sisters, were waiting in an old Model T. My grandmother had decided to leave her sons, maybe because the boarder was frightened they'd beat him up someday when they grew up. Uncle Mike and Dad stood by the coal furnace with a coin each in their hands. My uncle who was six had fifty cents; my father who was two had a quarter. They never saw her again, living or dead.

My father didn't talk about his past, the orphanage and the foster homes. And it struck me now that I would have liked to ask him about those hard years, for in some way they had made him the kind of man he was, living by a design known best to himself.

I watched the day dawn gold vermilion, like coals in a wood fire and remembered Sailor, take warning. I'd watched a lot of sunsets but not many dawns the last couple of years. I heard stirrings in the house. Sam's bedroom was on the ground floor. The smell of coffee brewing, like a creek bottom turned by the plow, wafted upstairs. There was a knock at the front door and then the remembered creak of its knurled pins and hinges followed by muffled words and steps ascending the carpeted stairs. The door handle turned. I watched it moving in the slow motion time of a man waking to something that he isn't sure isn't a dream. The woman who wheezed and shambled in was coal black, tall, fat, and wore oversized glasses shaped like cat's eyes. The name on her tunic was Pearline, like the Son House song. Behind her stood Sam in a tartan robe.

"And how is the General?" Pearline asked.

"Asleep," I said.

Her eyes rested on me briefly. Then she stooped noisily beside my father's bed; she took his pulse, touched his cheek. She looked at me and then at Sam.

"He's not asleep," she said. "He's passed."

17

When I looked at Sam, her eyes were swimming. And then I knew that mine were swimming too.

All the kin my father had left in the world, and that was Sam and I, stood beside him when they laid him down among the orchard of crosses in Robert E. Lee's peach orchard, a marble one now. Rags of snow lay strewn on the graves. The bugler was a red-headed Irishman named MacConcachee who looked too young to know "Taps," let alone play it. I flinched when they fired the guns and Sam took my hand. Holding on to each other we tottered towards the car; the earth seemed as shaky as a boat on rolling seas. The whole way home Sam cried in my arms in the back of the rented black Lincoln. She had loved my old man and it seemed a pity that a son whom he probably would not have chosen from a lineup of plausible applicants for the position was the last of his name and blood on this earth.

3. One Kind Favor

There's one kind favor I'll ask of you
See that my grave is kept clean.

Blind Lemon Jefferson

The first night my father lay in his grave I dreamed of Sam and Annie. In the dream a child again I stood just outside my bedroom at the head of the stairs. Halfway down them Sam was sitting with his arm around Annie looking into what should have been the living room. The foyer was flooded with music — Strauss, I think — and with brilliant, streaming light. Couples swept past the threshold between the foyer and the room of light and music. I could just glimpse a dress with flaring petticoats of red. As I slowly descended the curve of the staircase towards my brother and sister, I began to see the dancers. The staircase seemed to grow longer and longer as I took step after step, calling to Sam and Annie, never quite closing the distance between us.

The room beyond the foyer was immense, a bright cavern of music. Among the dancing couples I saw my father and mother. As they swept round and round they smiled into one another's eyes. I called out to them but they danced on. Then Sam turned to face me, his eyes wonderfully deep and brown and full of kindness. Even as I saw him alive I knew that he was dead. I yearned to touch him, not in the rough way of brothers but tenderly as I never remember having touched him in life. I called out to him again. But he had turned his face. Then he arose, and holding Annie's hand, he began to walk down the staircase towards the brilliant light. Her blond hair lay bunched in coils on the back of her sleeping pajamas, the one-piece kind with stocking feet. Just as I had to Sam, I called to her to stop. She turned and smiled at me, but she kept walking, the two of them receding before me like a tide gliding back to sea. I knew that if I did not catch them I would lose them forever. I began to run but I still could not reach them before they crossed the threshold of the room where the dancers whirled.

They walked hand in hand into the light towards my father and mother who had stopped dancing and who held out their arms in welcome. Gathering Annie to her breast, my mother lifted her for me to see, calling me to come. I ran towards them, though as before the distance between us never closed. A circle of strangers, their backs to me, arose between us, and I could not see beyond it. Though I called and called my family no longer seemed to hear me. I grew afraid. If I could break through the circle, I knew nothing would keep us apart forever. Now and then catching glimpse of Sam, now of

Annie, now of my mother. I walked round each way. Then I had a long clear view of my father. He was young again, the lines of pain gone from his face. His hands were on Sam's shoulders, Sam's back against his chest. Both of them looked at me, holding my eyes a long moment, then slowly they looked away.

Awake, I lay staring at the ceiling, certain that my brother was asleep in the bed in the corner of *our* room. I sat bolt upright and exchanged a long look with a dark bearded man. It took me a few seconds to grasp that what I was seeing was my own reflection.

I fell back on the bed like a swimmer collapsing on a beach after prolonged mortal struggle with the sea. Almost immediately I was asleep again, dreaming that I was swimming in the waters of Lake Atitlán. I had struck out for the opposite shore, and I was alone, the blue expanse of the lake mirror-calm around me. I could hear something bearing down fast. At last I saw it, no more than a gleaming speck. But with amazing speed, the speck became a red and white torpedo shape, trimmed with bright chrome. In an instant it was upon me, a huge propeller churning the water behind and on either side into a cauldron. On the side of the boat was written Chocomil. I dove down into the deep, clear azure, falling through layers of smoky water to escape the frantic blades. I began to gasp for air. I panicked, thrashing in the water, trying with all my strength to keep from breathing. Then I took a long drink.

I awoke in a coil of bedsheets, so drenched with sweat that I wondered for an instant from what world I had come. I rolled over on my side and for what seemed like hours watched the oyster-colored sky slowly become suffused with the neon colors of the dawn, calling me back from the land of dreams to the world where dreams never come true.

I knew where I was now. Yesterday they had buried my father. I lay in bed a long time thinking. I heard a car start up in the garage and remembered that Sam had said she had to go into school today, some loose ends to tie up. Glad to have the house to myself, I got up and dressed quickly in my old jeans and a ragged flight jacket. I grabbed a handful of bills from a stack of twenties Sam had given me the day before. Without bothering to shave or eat and with no clear destination in mind, I walked down the sidewalk until I found myself on a street corner. A bus stopped; I got on. The bus driver, a walrus of a man with the veiny, florid complexion of a hard drinker, an orange box of hair, and narrow, widely spaced teeth looked at me as if I were the kind of trouble he'd seen before and would just as soon not see again.

"Where to, Sir?" he asked, after a moment. He managed to put more provocation into the word Sir than if he'd called me a son of a bitch.

"Home," I said.

"What?" he asked.

"The zoo," I said.

I counted out the fare in change and staggered back to my seat as the bus lurched forward.

When the bus got to the Rock Creek Parkway, a long way from the zoo, I got out. The bus driver threw me a who cares look but I felt too absent-hearted to retaliate. I knew now where I wanted to go. A cold rain drizzled down on the clumps of rotten snow as I crossed the park through the woods, falling twice on the slick stones of the creek. Soon, it began to rain so hard that the creek water patches on my jeans didn't matter much. Then I got to a street corner where a stone church with walls of grey and brown fieldstone rubble stood surrounded by a low rusted iron picket fence. Below the short steeple roofed in copper crusted with verdigris was a weathered oak door studded with rosehead nails. It had been so long since I'd been there that I didn't remember the church's name and I didn't bother to look now. I did know the spot that I was seeking, out back and down below beside a drooping hemlock tree. My eyes on my feet, which cold as they were, I no longer seemed to feel; I walked slowly, until I got to the three headstones marking the graves: Sam, Mom, and Annie. All of them bore one date in common, a day in June I still hated to see come up on the calendar.

The last time I had come here had been twenty-five years ago. I had stood beside my father at just this spot, trying to make my face into a mirror of his. My eyes were trained on a yellow jacket that hovered above the flowers on my sister's casket, the smallest of the three. The clearest memory I have of that day is of that bright yellow and black striped torpedo landing on the box that contained Annie, who in my mind writhed, afraid that it would find a way inside, exploding her from her pretended sleep.

I went to stay with a friend that night, not one of mine, but of my dead brother's. My life had no more in common with this boy's than with Caroline Kennedy's. The next day he went to camp and I stayed on alone. Day after day I lay in bed staring at imaginary patterns in the whorled plaster of the ceiling. Then one day my Aunt Grace came, Uncle Mike's widow. She told me that my father had gone to Vietnam. Even as a boy of eight, I knew that meant he wouldn't be back for a long time. I lived at home next door to Aunt Grace with a housekeeper he had hired, an ascetic German lady with white blond hair. Taciturn but kind, Mrs. Flickinger lasted until Aunt Grace died and Sam came to live with us. When the General returned he seemed to have made a permanent break with the life of which my mother and brother and sister had been a part. I never heard him speak their names again and what made it stranger and sadder was that the pictures of my mother in the hallway became relics of a forgotten ancestor — more than if she had never been. Although Sam was named after my brother, even the way my father said her name was subtly different from the way he would have called my brother, as if there were a caesura in it, S-am, whereas he would have said my brother's name like a clap. Sam! It was as if with my mother, brother, and sister's deaths, I had been reborn suddenly at eight without a past, the boy I had been gone forever.

I don't know how long I stood there musing in the rain, soaked to the bone. I thought about them lying down there, not letting myself think about how they might look now. After a while I just let my mind go blank. A police car had pulled up beside the iron fence. The men inside were looking at me. I glanced up at them and went back to staring at the graves. My mind empty, I watched the little rivulets washing the clots of snow from the grass. When I looked up the police car had gone.

I stood there a long time in the rain. Then I began walking back towards the mall. I didn't know the names of the upscale streets I crossed, but I knew where I was headed. The few people who bothered to notice me looked quickly away. When I caught a glimpse of my reflection in a storefront window I understood. I looked near dead myself. All during that long trek I don't remember thinking about anything much, except that my feet had started to feel cold again. I was shivering a little now and I was ravenous. I stopped at a store whose windows were backed with iron bars. The name on the door was something Korean. There was a doll-like Asian woman sitting behind a cash register surrounded by what I guessed was bullet proof glass. I must have looked like the same trouble to her that I did to everyone else because she called out to somebody in the back and a young man who might have been her son came out and stood nervously beside her, his hand fingering something underneath the counter. When I thought about it later, I reckoned it had probably been a gun.

I bought a grape soda, some salted peanuts and a Moon Pie with one of the twenties. Shoving the change in my pocket without counting it, I left with a little brown bag in my left hand.

None of the food I'd bought tasted like much, but I didn't shiver after I finished the Moon Pie. A long, long time it was I walked. Then I found myself at Pennsylvania Avenue looking at the National Gallery of Art. I crossed the street and went in. The guards didn't look at me especially. I guess they were used to street people. I walked towards the big room with the two Rembrandt self-portraits, the ones in which you get the feeling that he painted his own face as if he were painting someone else's and was surprised by what he saw there. I liked the older face of Rembrandt better. It's a silly face really, with the big clown's nose and the putty chin, a face whose grandeur is all in the eyes. The eyes return your stare unappalled by vicissitude, by faded reputation, by times hard and poor, by mortality itself. It started me thinking about Robert Johnson whose life, though short, had cut him to the bone. I could hear his voice in my mind. Stones in my passway, my road seem black as night.

Sodden but warmed, I walked back up Independence towards the General's house, sometime after two. I bought a copy of the *Post* from a vending machine and stopped off at the Tune Inn. I got the booth across from the stuffed fox head, and ordered a hamburger, a pack of Camel shorts, and a pitcher of dark beer. I read about the Redskins, who as usual were beat to hell by injuries, and about why the Native Americans wanted them to change the team's name to something politically correct. Then I read *Calvin and Hobbes* and *Ernie* and *The Fusco Brothers*. It was good to laugh a little. While I was on the funnies page, I glanced at my horoscope; there was something about study Aries message. To hell with that, I thought. Then I turned to the death notices and froze when I saw my name, or rather my old man's. I couldn't read the obituary; instead, I ripped it out and put it in my pocket. I set the paper down and drank most of a pitcher of beer and smoked cigarette after cigarette just staring out the window at the rain. Then I went back to reading. There had been three murders in Washington the day before, one of the dead was a three-year-old girl shot in a playground. I read all about that. I never did get to the front page.

I was on my third pitcher of beer when, dark falling, they started to come in, the women wearing their hair Garbo short, but parted on one side, and the men in white sidewall haircuts topped with dark thatches. Both sexes smoked menthol cigarettes and wore baggy clothes, white socks, Nike or Reebok running shoes and Rolexes. Not all of them dressed exactly alike, of course, but enough did that you got the impression that there was a look that went with the turf and I was certain I didn't have it. Or want it for that matter. I got up, paid my bill, and walked home.

Standing at the General's door about to knock I heard a piano, and listening for a minute, I recognized *Claire de Lune*. I'd never much cared for DeBussy but the old man had liked that piece. Just to please him, Sam had learned it when she was young. I walked around the side of the house to the den and looked in through the French doors. The walls were lined with bookshelves, for the General had been a great reader: He was not one to buy a book as an ornament. He'd liked history — you'd have expected that — but he'd liked the Russians too; he had a special fondness for Nabokov's translation of *A Hero of our Time*.

Sam was seated at the piano, a big mahogany Steinway, tears streaming down her face. She was all heart, that girl. I knew that I was watching something that I would remember as long as I lived and I didn't want to rush the moment. She played well and she played long. When she stopped, she sat there a while, staring at the piano. Then she stood up, closed the cover over the keys and walked out of the room. I didn't want her to see me, not the way I looked, not the way she felt, so I walked back down to Independence. I had the walking blues, thinking about Sam, feeling like blowing my lonesome horn. I passed up the Tunes and the Gay Blade, whose name advertised its clientele. I ended up buying a coke at another Korean convenience store and sitting on a bench in the Metro station till I felt sober enough to go home. On the way back I looked in again at the Tunes. The young professional set with the Euro-trash detailing had spent their happy hour there and gone on. I felt sober enough to get drunk again and I still had a couple of Sam's twenties. I gave the glass door a shove and walked in.

"What can I get yez?" A rough looking Irishman was tending bar. His face and red hair reminded me of the bugler from North Tonawanda. I put a twenty down on the bar and covered it with my hand.

"Jim Beam," I said. "Three shots shaken with ice and poured neat."

I didn't get home that night until late. Sam was asleep, though she'd left her door open and her nightlight on.

I stumbled up the stairs, hitting the walls a couple of times, trying to keep my balance. Sam had left a light on for me by the bed, the one my old man dad died in.

Drink deep, dream deep. After that half hour at the French window it's not surprising what I dreamed. I was riding in a flesh colored car, everything in it and on it was the color of flesh. Sam was driving, not a stitch on. I was dressed for the woods in a shirt of red and black checked wool, high boots, lumberjack pants. We were driving in the mountains where my cabin is. Then Sam stopped the car and smiled at me. I was struck by wonder; I hadn't seen her naked since she was a little girl. Sam didn't seem to notice. She walked with that elegance that tall women have, barefoot, head up, arms lifted. It was late fall and the bare branches were hung with a scattering of leaves. The forest floor was covered with them, flattened down as if by rain. We made no sound walking, I a little behind her and off to one side, almost as if I were filming her. She talked to me as you would talk to a child, or as if she too were a child and had brought me to these woods to show me something, a secret. We had come to a level place in the deep woods. She was telling me the names of trees. We came to a big granddaddy poplar, and she showed me its bark, deeply scored and lichen-covered. There were morels at the foot of it shaped like little brains, except that instead of being the color of coffee grounds, they were flame red.

She took me then to an oak, enormous, gnarled, with sweeping branches that shot straight up at the ends, a field tree that after centuries had found itself again part of a forest and sent its branches searching for the sun. Sam was smiling at me but she held herself aloof. Then suddenly I stopped. Before me was a tree unlike any I had ever seen, much shorter than the tall straight forest trees, its spreading branches shaped like the lobes of a human brain. The trees around it were nearly bare, but this tree had all of its leaves. It was these that had arrested me. Each leaf was huge, larger than a human face, almost as large as my chest and flame red, not orange but scarlet, shaped like a heart, except that its edges were serrated like the leaf of a briar. Sam had moved on. I called out to her and she walked back towards me very calm, still speaking with the detachment of someone giving lessons.

What is this tree I asked her.

She looked at me. Suddenly her face was so close, I could see the golden flecks in her iris.

This, she said, is the Komodo Dragon Tree of Love.

24

I awoke, certain that the dream had revealed to me only what I long had known: that kimono or komodo, dragon or dragon tree, heart or brain, tree of life or tree of doom, it was Sam I loved, had loved, was fated to love till I died. Then I did something I have never done before: I wrote the dream down on a piece of loose-leaf notebook paper, the kind with holes for a binder. All of it, just as I remembered it. The skies were still dark. I got up and walked down to the den, slipping the paper between the covers of the same sheet music. Then I came up and went to bed. I slept soundly till noon.

That same evening I heard Sam playing DeBussy again. Suddenly she stopped. I lay in bed a long time listening to nothing at all, sleepless, dreaming. The next morning as I ate breakfast she walked in and sat down at the table; I caught her looking at me as I set my coffee down. We exchanged a long look, our faces blank. Neither of us said a word. I got up and put my plate and cup in the dishwasher. I poured her a cup of coffee and kissed her on the cheek. Then I got my coat and went out. It was after midnight when I got home from the Tunes. She'd left lights burning to light my way to bed, but I only made it as far as the landing. Sometime towards dawn, she got me up and helped me into bed. I dreamed that she kissed me on the lips and said she loved me too.

4. Don't My Gal Look Good

Don't that cloud look lonesome coming cross the deep blue sea,
and don't my gal look good, coming after me.

Leroy Carr

The next week I spent at home with Sam trying to resolve my father's estate. She was his executor, a wise choice given the alternative. She had taken a leave of absence from her job teaching second grade in McLean when the General's cancer had been found. As always, there was also someone in love with her, a lawyer with the firm that handled the General's legal affairs. The size of the ring she wore indicated that he was serious, conventional, and probably rich. Once in a while I heard the trailing end of his telephoned importunings as Sam fended him off. Drying out as best I could in anticipation of the semester ahead, I was in no mood for tea and sympathy with Charley-Boy, as I took to referring to Sam's young man. I didn't want to meet him or to acknowledge that he existed. But I could see Sam wanted us to meet, and I owed her that much.

My antipathy, it turned out, was preternaturally apt. Charles D. Bledsoe, a stalwart paladin of capitalism and lawyerdom, had the excellent good fortune, for which I hated him heartily, of not being Sam's almost cousin. Charley-Boy was about my age and even looked a little like me, but not so scuffed and dinged. To enhance the resemblance, or so I flattered myself, Sam had encouraged him to grow a beard and the result was an effect as manicured and artificial as a plucked eyebrow. I think he hated me on first sight as much as I hated him, but he was smart enough to play his cards close to his vest, knowing that I was Sam's favorite lost cause.

Bledsdoe had a failed marriage behind him. *No kids* he informed me in italics. The world was better off for whatever contraceptive gizmo had spared us his iteration. Then there were his tastes and prejudices. Bledsdoe was a diehard Reaganite; raved about the over-the-hill voice of Sinatra; had actually reread a Robert Ludlum novel; drank white wine; mentioned a family home "on the Cape" four times in twenty minutes; wore tasseled patent leather loafers; drove a BMW; had graduated Dartmouth and "read law" at Harvard; owned a spiffy town house in Georgetown; belonged to a health club; ordered bottled water with his white wine and called it a spritzer; subscribed to *The Wall Street Journal* and *Playboy* and *Vanity Fair*; disliked *The Post*; preferred Eisenhower to Truman; and said he had never heard of Robert Johnson. It figured that the General had actually liked this piece of shit. I decided that if I got drunk enough I could get away with insulting him, but I didn't. Sam would only respect him the more for not insulting me back. Probably she would mistakenly attribute this restraint to his character instead of to the habit of that circumspect profession which kept his purse lined. As I consumed the expensive French dinner that Charley-Boy had staked me to, I tried to see me from his side: the almost cousin, a disappointment to his father, a burnt-out ne'er-do-well, a refugee from a bad marriage who left it to others to clean up his messes, a drunk, who smoked unfiltered Camels, a holier-than-thou spent bullet of a liberal democrat, guarding the gates to Charley Bledsoe's proposed sojourn in Eden with Samantha Callaghan, the leggy beauty who would shine as his corporate consort and bear the children of his lawyer's loins: Yes, I tried to see it from his side, but it only made me want to throw Sam over my shoulder and make a run for the border.

"So, Jack," he said in a phony Harvard accent. "What in God's name did you do in whatever place it was, Guatemala? Yes, Guatemala. For two years? I mean, what does anyone do in a godforsaken place like that?"

"Everything I set out to," I said, blowing a cloud of smoke straight at him which he tried unsuccessfully to dodge.

"What was that?" He had this thin-lipped, supercilious, waspier-than-thou smile that managed to convey an insulting and completely unearned superiority.

"To go native," I said.

"Native?" he asked.

"See that?" I tapped my nostril. "The hole was for the little bone that went through my nose."

Sam giggled. She was a little tight. She sidled over and hugged me, kissing me on the cheek.

Charley-Boy's face had taken on a *Doctor Strangelove* quality, as though he was trying to weather an attack of tooth pain while smiling into the camera. Enjoying my role as dental probe, I hugged Sam back and kissed her chastely but noisily, like you'd kiss a baby. The bulging deep-sea creature gleam in Charley's eyes throbbed with a nearly audible pain.

"So you wasted two years of your life leaving your father and Sam to pick up the pieces."

"What pieces?"

Sam shot Charley a "Not Now" look and she began irrelevantly to regale us with an account of her experiences the summer before at some summer camp for kids from the D.C. projects. A succession of neat whiskies had begun to slow down my thinking and thicken my speech. I've never been belligerent when blotto, modeling myself on the original literary wasp, Beowulf: "Drunk, he slew no hearth companions." Even Charley, though

27

hardly qualifying as a hearth companion, had begun in my estimation to take on sterling qualities like solvency, particularly the ability to stake me to a half bottle of bourbon at ten dollars an inch. We were both looking at Sam when generous feelings began to well up as I reached for another double. Sam cocked her head skeptically to take me in. I raised my glass and winked at her.

"Well," I said, "here's to Sam, and any man she graces with her hand."

There was confusion on Sam's face and phony delight on Charley's. Without meaning to, I'd scored a palpable hit.

"I'm not married yet," Sam said. And I noticed for the first time she wasn't wearing the ring.

"Oh," I said intelligently.

"Well," Charley said, "I'm still the front runner, eh, Sam?"

Sam's smile was noncommittal. Having created this contretemps, I excused myself and goose-stepped off to the lobby, mistaking it for the hallway to the men's room. I compounded my mistake and strode brilliantly through the revolving doors onto the sidewalk.

It was a clear, cold night, the stars so bright you could almost hear them shining like a symphony of icicles. My benevolence intensified as my sense of balance diminished. I found myself hugging a young elm more as a prop than as homage to Kilmer. From nowhere I fished a line of Whitman:

"A mouse is miracle enough to stagger sextillions of infidels."

The goofy hyperbole of this line had prompted me to hilarity as an undergraduate but it seemed a noble sentiment now.

"A mouse" I said in parody of the forensic Richard Burton—"is miracle enough." Now I was sonorous. Ralph Richardson "To stagger"—spooky, wide-eyed John Carradine —"Sextillions"—the thrashing snake of Olivier in the last scene of the movie of *Richard III* "Of Infidels." Gielgud as the somber Prospero.

I turned and saw Sam smiling at me. She was leaning against the wall of the restaurant, her arms folded across her breast. When I stopped, I smiled what felt like, numb as I was, a lopsided grin. Through the door I glimpsed Charley-Boy at the threshold of the coat check room. He was staring peevishly into the dining area, one patent leather foot tapping, its tassel flying.

Very slowly Sam walked over to me. When she touched my face with her hand I kissed her palm and looked at her with what felt like all the hopeless longing of that moonless night of icicle stars.

"I love you, Sam," I said.

I never meant to say it, not like that. The look on her face — I shall never forget it — was radiant. She reached down into my coat and pulled the lapels up and smoothed them. Then she leaned forward and kissed me on the soft part of my ear.

For me the trip home was suffused with the inarticulate promise of that kiss. The bourbon-bemused fog between my ears began to dissipate. It was early, perhaps nine, perhaps a little later. Sam asked Charley Boy to drive us over the Fourteenth Street Bridge. Take us round the beltway, she said. She opened her window, flooding the back seat of the car where I was sitting with what felt like a blast straight from Alberta. Are you cold Jackie? She asked me. I don't remember whether I said I was or I wasn't. I was looking directly into her eyes. I'm trying to wake you up, she said. Let me feel your cheek. Charley-Boy's eyes, narrow with impatience, flashed at me in the rear view mirror. He was a prince among men. In my mood Mussolini was a prince among men. Sam touched my cheek. I brushed her fingertips with my lips. She stroked my moustache. I kept smiling wider and wider until it felt like my face was all teeth. Sam reached into her pocket book. She put on Bonnie Raitt: "Nick of Time." It was the right song for the moment. I felt like one of those electric oil-filled radiators, as if some hand (Sam's!) was slowly turning up the dial. She smiled at me, crinkling up the corners of her eyes.

"You better take us home," she said, looking straight at me, "I need to put Jackie to bed."

My heart was racing. It was somewhere ahead of the Beamer's hood ornament, streaming towards home, while inside with the cold wind bracing me up I sat grinning, a George Dickel Buddha.

When we got to my father's house I made a quick goodbye. I wasn't sure what Sam was going to do. I must have walked slowly because by the time I reached the door Sam with her long-legged strides was right behind me. I didn't have the key. I heard the Beamer rev twice as Charley-Boy double-clutched into reverse.

Sam was looking at me as if she wanted to swim right into my eyes. When we entered the house, I reached for the light and her hand covered mine. No, she said. Kiss me, Jack. I turned to face her. The glass side panel door with the fan of glass overhead threw a moony shadow into the hallway of light borrowed from street lamps. I could make out the shape of her hair, a flicker of eye-gleam. I could smell the wine on her mouth before I tasted it. I didn't kiss her deep, I didn't want to rush the moment. My hand had dropped to her hip and she pressed it in answer. It was a long kiss.

She led me to her room. It wasn't what the General would have called ready for inspection. One tall boot, bent halfway up stood beside the bed. The pulled-out drawers of her dresser formed a kind of crazy staircase to the mirror where I could see her reflection, and my own.

"Take off your coat, Jack."

I took it off.

"Lie down."

"Where?" I asked.

"On the bed." She pushed me down.

Some sense of the enormity of what we were about to do gave me a scintilla of hesitation.

"Cousin Sam — "

She put her finger on my lips.

"Sh-Sh, Jackie."

"Sam — "

"I know. I know."

She was on top of me, kissing me. She got me out of my shirt. I heard a button pop. Sam giggled.

"Oh, oh." She kissed me. "I guess I'll have to do some sewing tomorrow."

"I reckon I'll have to do some sowing myself, tonight." I said. "I'm fixing to hook up my plow right now."

She lay back and laughed at this and then sighed.

"Stay put."

I wasn't going anywhere. She reached over me and turned on the Cowboy Junkies. Then she stood up. Her dress rustled up and over with a noise like wind in the leaves. She stood in a shaft of light, her exposed breasts full and round. She shook her hair out of the last bit of braid that had entwined it. She had a long back, full buttocks and long full legs. Then she sighed a melody of longing and requital. She knelt over me and threw her head back and began to rock back and forth. Then she bent down and kissed me, holding my tongue in her mouth while she moved her hips in a rhythm like the sea lapping the shore as the tide rose slowly, enveloping us both.

5. Me and the Devil

Early this morning, you knocked upon my door.

And I said hello Satan, I believe it's time to go.

Robert Johnson

When I awoke, Sam was asleep in the curl of my chest. A strand of her hair stretched across into her mouth. We had gotten to sleep only towards dawn. My arm was draped across her hip, brown and hairy as a coconut. Her own skin was white and lightly freckled, covered in almost invisible swirls of hair.

For a long time I lay there watching her as she slept. You lucky son of a bitch, I said to myself. Don't fuck this up, Jack. You'll never find another one like her again. I bent my face to hers, kissing her on the cheek. Nobody had ever been that beautiful ever, anywhere on earth. I drifted awhile in thought until I found myself thinking that on Wednesday I would drive in the General's Lincoln, the one with the suicide doors, down to Charlottesville. I savored in anticipation the delicious moment when I would hail Vandillingham at the threshold of his office. It would ruin his whole day. It would be the making of mine. Later I would have to canvass the English department to gauge the extent to which my colleagues shared the chairman's opinion of me. The caboose to this train of thought was that I was going to have to meet Donna. Before I left the country I had signed the check for the settlement our lawyers had concocted to get us free of one another. The last thing I had done before bolting was to leave a signed copy of the agreement with my lawyer, Rucker Breeden, a college roommate and one of the many whom Donna had bedded before she laid her snare for me.

I turned my face to the real thing. Against the long odds of my suitability as anything more than a one-night stand, I asked myself whether there was still a chance for a spent bullet like me? Well maybe not quite spent. I brushed her cheek with my lips.

"Sam." I said. She stirred and rubbed her leg against my front.

"Baby," she said. Then she turned to face me, wrapping her arms about my neck and her legs around my hips.

Later that morning we drove to Leo McCardell's office in the Continental, whose engine ran like a sewing machine and was cleaner than most people's toasters. Sam sat right beside me, smiling, radiant, her hand touching me on the shoulder, the knee. I stopped at every light, green, red, or

31

yellow, looking into her eyes. Idiot, she said, kissing me. Horns followed us blaring rage, importuning us with all the tension of the mundane. I never felt such euphoria. There had been a couple of good months somewhere with Donna of sex exalted by chemicals. Maybe that was what this was too, a riot of the hormones playing the muzak of the glands. But it had been so long since I'd felt this good that I was beyond caring to know. I was depraved enough or amoral enough or smart enough just to live it.

Leo McCardell, the General's lawyer and longtime crony looked like a pirate gone to seed. He lost one eye to shrapnel in World War II and he wore a black eye patch which didn't fit his geriatric wardrobe of off-the-rack suits a couple of sizes too big at the shoulder and about the same number of sizes too small at the gut. He'd always hated shaving and yet couldn't quite give himself over to anything as heterodox as a beard. The result was a sort of salt-and-pepper mold that he hacked off his face every Sunday. This being Monday, his face looked like he'd dipped it into the cuisinart. He and the General had flown Spitfires together in the R.C.A.F. before Pearl Harbor and they'd stayed friends. Usually Leo left clients to junior partners like Bledsoe. It was only because he had soldiered with my father that Sam and I were admitted to his inner sanctum. Charley was busy in court.

Leo hugged Sam wholeheartedly and shook my hand with a look of bemused disapproval. His shrewd lawyer's eye sized up Sam's radiance and determined pretty quickly it wasn't in anticipation of the General's posthumous largess.

"Well, Jack," he said, "if it makes any difference to you, you're a rich man."

I nodded, thinking, "Inherit a great fortune, inherit a great misfortune."

"Not much" is what I said.

"A million and a quarter is a good sized jingle in your pocket, Jack."

"I guess it won't change my life much," I said. How the hell do I know that? I thought.

"No," he said, "the way you live, probably not."

The General's holographic will was succinct and spare, written in his characteristically neat slanting print-script. Besides money and stock, he left me the house and cars. Sam's inheritance at Aunt Grace's death which had come to her at twenty-one already had made her financially independent, but the General had left her my mother's collection of china and a half million.

"Your wife, Jack, made some claims against you which your father settled while you were on your travels.

"My ex-wife?"

"She wasn't then."

"If she isn't, she will be," I said.

Again Leo threw an appraising look at Sam and then at me.

"There's something else."

I looked at him. Melodrama and lawyers, I thought, don't mix well.

"Using me — actually, Charley Bledsdoe — as your agent, your father bought your land and cabin when your ex-wife put it up for sale. It comes to you free and clear."

"My cabin?"

I hadn't let myself think about losing the cabin in two years. Every time it would come into my mind I'd turn it off like a light switch. The old man had known I loved it and had saved it for me. He loves you, Jack, Sam had said to me the first night I got back. Suddenly for the first time in what felt like centuries I thought of him as a father trying to mend fences with his son.

I got up. I needed to take a bit of a walk to collect myself. Leo suggested an office down the hall. I ended up walking to the elevator and taking it down to the ground floor. The doorman, whose uniform looked like a pastiche of bits left over from the Crimean war, let me out with a soldierly nod.

"Sorry about your father, Mr. Shock," he said.

I must have looked at him oddly because he went on.

"I knew your father ... in Thailand during the war."

"Yes. During the war."

"Vietnam. He was a great man."

"Thanks." I went out.

A great man. I'd never really seen my father as even an everyday man, let alone as a great one. As a father I had judged him and found him wanting. All my life he had been my adversary. He had wanted to make me tougher than the blows of fate. Now that he was gone, there was no one left to take his place. Except that part of him that I had internalized. Like him I'd never learned to live with anyone. Two years ago, a solitary drunken paladin, I'd gone sailing off melodramatically into the sunset towards Central America, masking the wounds with a cosmetically straight back, just as he had when my mother and brother and sister had died. My face as I caught my reflection in the window was the very image of my father's: wary, skeptical, brooding, detached.

Just then Sam walked out the door. She stood stock still taking me in.

"Are you all right, Jack?"

"Yes."

"It was pretty wonderful of your dad to buy the cabin."

33

I dropped my eyes and spoke falteringly, "Never thought the old man cared enough to care for anything I cared for."

"He loved you, Jack."

Somehow this didn't comfort me, for I wasn't sure I'd ever love him back, even now.

"What are you going to do?" she asked.

"You mean about school?"

"Well, you'll go down to school. I know that."

"Yes."

"But what about you and me, Jack."

"Sam," I said, "I love you."

"I know."

My voice had gotten thick and halting, and like my old man I hated myself for all this feeling, even as I knew that it was just this that made me what I was, made Sam love me.

She came over and put her hand on my cheek. I kissed her wrist.

"Sam …"

She smiled at me.

"Will you marry me?"

"Tonight?" She was smiling wider.

"Tonight, I've got covered."

"How about tomorrow morning?"

"I've got that covered too."

"When will you drive down to Charlottesville?"

"Classes start on Thursday."

She laughed. "Old Doc Shock. Tardy as usual."

"That's me. Do we need to see McCardell again?"

"No. He'll send us some papers to sign." We started walking to the Continental.

"What about you?"

"I have to start teaching too."

"When?"

"Friday."

"Why didn't you tell me?"

34

"Jack, you know me and dates."

"Like me and dates, only worse." We were getting in the car.

"You know me so well."

I smiled. "I do," I said. We sat there a while.

"Will you marry me?"

She looked at me. "Oh, Jack. I don't know."

"You know."

"Yes. I know." She kissed me. "I love you, Jack."

"How much?"

"Too much."

She reached out to touch my cheek. I kissed her fingers.

"I've got to leave for Charlottesville early in the morning," I said, though Sam already knew this.

"There'll be plenty of time for tomorrow." She leaned over and kissed me. It was a long slow kiss that drained me down and pumped me up.

"You're a good kisser, Sam."

"Get me home, Doctor Shock." She winked at me.

"Female Trouble again?" I asked.

"Nothing you can't handle," she said.

I awoke with the false dawn. Sam was asleep, her back curved into my chest. She was breathing heavily and slowly. For a while I lay there listening to her, watching her face. I kissed her cheek. She stirred. "Jackie," she said.

"Do you love me, Sam?" I asked her again.

"Un-huh."

I lay there a long time watching her sleep. I didn't want anything bad to happen to her. And I wondered if I was what I needed to protect her from. On the wall above her bed there was a picture of her sitting on the backyard swing wearing an Indian headband and holding a little bow and arrow in her hand. I couldn't really see it in the gloom, but I knew it was there. I had taken that picture of Sam with a little Vivitar soon after her sixth birthday. I remembered when she had moved in with us when I was twelve. She was barely four. For me it was love at first sight. She was like a puppy, only better, with her big smile and laughing, blue eyes. I'd helped Rena, the sweet old black lady who took care of us, to put her to bed, to make her lunch and to walk her to school. I'd taught her to ride a bike, checked her homework. Once when my teacher Mrs. Reardon had asked us in class to list all the people we loved, I wrote down Sam first, without hesitating, then Rena and my dog Bill and my cat Biddy. My father hadn't made the list at all.

All the catastrophes, the deaths of my mother and brother and sister, of my uncle and aunt, had had the effect of deadening or at least submerging my capacity to feel much, except for Sam. I was in college when Sam began to pass through the rites of puberty, boys and bras and makeup.

In college the girls I dated were hot bloods. They tended to be breezily promiscuous like Donna or sexually conflicted like Sarah, another girl I had loved, and whom occasionally, because I was crazy about her, rather than because I liked it much, I sometimes shared in bed with another woman who liked women better than men, though not entirely instead of men. Both Donna and Sarah had been blonds with muddy green or hazel eyes. To me that look was still the image of sexual desire, just as Sam with her fair skin and black hair and clear blue eyes and radiant smile was the image of that hackneyed phrase sweetness and light.

That had all changed one night when I drove up from school with Donna on a weekend when the General was on TDY out west. Sam was supposed to be staying with a friend. Donna and I were on the stairs almost to the bedroom door when we heard the unmistakable sounds of sex. Donna smiled at me. "Sounds like little Sam is losing her cherry." She kicked off her shoes and stepped out of her panties. "Fuck me on the stairs, Jack."

I pushed her aside and bolted up the stairs, throwing myself against my own bedroom door. Two chiaroscuro figures moved to one rhythm in the dark. I grabbed the top figure by the hair and stood him up, punching him in the gut so hard he sucked wind.

Donna had turned on the light. She was laughing.

"Hey, Sam, is this guy any good?" But it wasn't Sam. It was her friend Gina del Florio. She was screaming "Jesus! Jesus! Jesus!" Donna was laughing; the guy had the dry heaves. I felt sick at the brutality of what I'd done but I made no amends. I rushed past the door, past Donna, down the stairs to the door of Sam's bedroom. She wasn't there. Maniacally I started pulling out her drawers, and in one of them I found a little dial of birth control pills. Three of them were gone. I sat down on her bed hyperventilating. Donna had followed me down. You've really got a thing for that cousin of yours, haven't you? She was walking towards me unbuttoning her sweater. Behind her through the open door I saw the boy leaving with Gina supporting him. So let's do it here, Donna said. In Sam's room. She was putting on some of the perfume that Sam used. Fuck me, Jack, she said. I'm Sam. I toppled her onto Sam's bed and lifted her skirt. I think I almost hated her at that moment but I never felt so hard as when I entered her. Afterwards I lay back next to her staring up at the ceiling. Poor Jackie, she said. Sick and twisted, she laughed, turning towards me. She grabbed my cock. Hard again she said, just the way I like you.

6. A Kind Hearted Woman

I got a kind hearted woman
She studies evil all the time.
You well's to kill me
As to have it on your mind.

Robert Johnson

Donna Gordon Prileau. Empress of Bitchery. Mirror of my own obsession with sex. Exploiter of my genius for catastrophe. A Botticelli face, grey green eyes a little askew, the sweet small red mouth made for lies and lovemaking. She was a year older and a class above me when I met her. Making the rounds of the dope-smoking coked-out musicians in the night scene, she'd broken some hearts and fucked up some heads. And she was clearly getting off on it.

Homecoming 1976, the Tri Delt House. Bored, stoned Jack Shock, slide guitar player for the Terraplanes, looking for Suzie Creamcheese among the glassy eyed college girls in tight dresses who used each other like bird dogs to point out who they would roll and tumble that night. Then I saw her.

Two thin braids on either side of her face, long honey blonde hair, skin the same color on arms and legs that looked too good to be real, smiling wide, mouth open a little. The band had gone on break and I was playing Blind Willie Johnson "Dark was the Night, Cold was the Ground, the Day My Savior Died," a prophecy, if only I had known it then, of my marriage. The song had nothing to do with why she was looking at me — her eyes, the tilt of her body, her smile — all telegraphing that she was there, that I could have her, and that she'd make sure I liked what I came for. I knew she'd slept with Rucker with the casual promiscuity the cool affected in the seventies, but that fact didn't have the cock blocking effect that it should have. No, I didn't flinch that night when she told me that she'd gotten to Rucker to get to me. I felt flattered. After I met her father, I felt fated. He was a land developer from Mobile and I looked like a younger version of the daddy that had spoiled her rotten.

Before I met Donna, I cloaked sex in an English major's idealism: "For God's sake hold your tongue and let me love," and all that. Any illusion I had that Donna was a kindred spirit went out the window soon enough. She had it bad for me all right, but I had it even worse for her. The Jack Shock I was back then really did love the girl. Shallow Jack, sucker for a beautiful face, a woman's body, a mind alive with games. She made it her business to know me through and through, and she came after me with a singleness of purpose that no one else had ever shown. Yes, I was infatuated, obsessed, call it what you want to. And that first night when she took me to her room, I remember thinking as she touched her tongue to the head of my cock and smiled at me that I'd have probably set myself on fire if she'd asked me to.

I don't doubt that Donna wasn't lying when she said she loved me as much as she had ever loved anyone. As for bonehead me, I couldn't even imagine life without her. But then I didn't know much back then. Least of all about Jack Shock. The night before graduation, she asked me if I wanted to make an honest woman out of her. We were standing in a rose garden beside a serpentine wall on the East Range. I told her I didn't want her honest, I wanted her bad. A year later we were married in one of those enormous Southern weddings that begin a week before the vows and end with a cruise to an island in the Caribbean.

From the beginning our love fed on jealousy, fights, parties, stormy partings. But Donna knew she had my undivided attention and at first that was enough. When I was accepted into graduate school at Chapel Hill, the donkey work of the doctoral program replaced the melodrama of adrenaline rushes. Once I started my dissertation, she started staying out late. I didn't blame her. She was nobody's idea of Penelope. Then I caught her in bed with my Faulkner professor. When I say "caught," what I mean is I was the prey, not him. It was my comeuppance. We reconciled, but it was never the same for me after that. One thing troubled me more and more as time went on. In all the years I lived with her I never saw Donna commit a single act of disinterested kindness.

Once we'd moved back to Charlottesville and I was thoroughly enmeshed in the routine of teaching and work on the book, Donna began selling real estate to supplement Daddy Prileau's allowance, a sum already several thousand dollars more than my salary. Before long she found her way into the horsey set, riding to hounds with Farmington and cruising the town nights in her pink convertible Beamer, another gift from Mobile. I had ceased to care whether she was cheating on me or not. All that remained between us towards the end was sex. You know how it goes: The more I hated her the more I wanted her. Night by night we sweated wordlessly in each other's arms, except for the little cries Donna gave as the transports gripped her about ten minutes into coitus. You could have set your clock by them.

God knows how long our joke of a marriage would have lasted if I hadn't walked in on her fucking one of her horsey clients on the kitchen butcher block. I didn't know I had it in me but I kicked him in his naked balls and cut off his ponytail with the bread knife buried in a cutting board by the sink. I dragged him by the ears to the living room and sent him out by the window. Then I helped Donna, also starkers, find the door, and urged her Beamer on its way with some sharp heel kicks which I used to recontour the fenders. I never let her in the house again. The next day I rented the biggest U-

Haul I could find and moved everything except my clothes and books into it. It sat there for eleven days until I found the apartment where she and horsey boy were staying. I drove the truck over to her new address, parked it, taped the truck key to her windshield and left it there blocking the Beamer, now restored to its epicene splendor. This melodramatic gesture cost me four hundred and seventy dollars in U-Haul fees, but by then I was done with her. I'd had my fill of *Death Wish Revisited*. There was one false step, I nailed her on her office desk after we talked — argued — over the settlement. That was the last tango in C'ville for Donna and me. We went back to fighting over the property. The sticking point was the cabin I'd built over two summers in Nelson County. I wouldn't agree to let her have it. Meanwhile, her ponytailess lover, a rich cokehead named Dabney Wimbish had run out on his wife and two kids. Later, after his life was good and wrecked, Donna kicked him out, and rented a place a block down the street from our old house. There she made a stab at the role of the aggrieved but forgiving spouse. To judge by the changing stream of cars that soon appeared at all hours of the night and morning, she tired of the part quickly. She had no trouble recruiting stand-ins. She still had her looks, all in the bones and skin. She looked better, if anything, than when I'd married her. And she made sure I knew it. Dropping by with a new lover in tow with an offer to share some Remy or cocaine. Declined, without thanks. Calling me from her bed while she carried on a nuts-and-bolts conversation with her lover of the moment on sexual technique. Subtlety was not Donna's long suit.

The final ploy in her strategy to bring me to my knees was the pursuit and capture of my chief rival for tenure and best friend. In the best post-modern way Bill Smalls, a Shakespeare scholar, yoked Foucault to the bard in a series of articles later published as a book. I can still remember some of the chapter titles, because I read and edited the manuscript. "Hamlet on the Battlements: Linguistics as End Game"; "The Black Man's Burden: The phenomenology of enslavement in *Othello*"; "Apocalypse Now? *Coriolanus:* a Structuralist reading"; "Lear as Lacan: the syntax of insanity." Bill's work was hardly cutting edge. He was shrewd enough to see that the University didn't really want to be identified as *avant-garde*. In spite of an acute case of Harvarditis, Bill's symptoms being namedropping and an unconvincing broad "A," I liked Smalls because he loved books: he could quote whole passages of the plays. That and a willingness to talk unguardedly about ideas was what kept us friends in a department where colleagues saw colleagues as Machiavellis and Mata Haris ready to steal their "big ideas" at every cocktail throng. Smalls' wife, tiny Betsey with her huge blue eyes, and Nev and Casey, boy and girl twins, were the family I told myself I wished I had. Tall, stick-thin with a boy's skin and dark hair, looking with his thin-rimmed spectacles a little like Dennis the Menace's dad, Bill was a friend who actually followed through on his offers to help, and who treated me with an affection that belied our status as rivals for the tenure-track job that we believed awaited one of us at the end of eight years of ill-paid, hard-slogging anxiety.

Actually, both of us took for granted that no real rivalry existed since the department had hired me only in response to a demand from Richmond for a folklorist with an African-American concentration. I was the only plausible candidate on the stage that year. No one seriously entertained the notion that I'd actually be given any kind of permanent position. For one thing I wasn't African-American. For another, almost nobody in the department had even heard of Robert Johnson: certainly they didn't consider my interest in him evidence of serious scholarship. I don't like to think it now, and I never consciously processed it then, but maybe the reason that Bill stayed my friend through my drinking and laconic despair during those years was that he took for granted what everyone else did, that I'd go up or down in flames on scaffold day, a wisp in the Coral Sea of that good oblivion to which the department commended the souls of those graduate students and assistant professors who fell short of its standards. I'm sure that when my book came out a couple of years before doomsday, as we privately referred to our rendezvous at some disputed barricade with the tenure committee, Bill's happiness at it and the reviews it got was sincere enough. Some generous praise by a soon-to-die Agrarian of the Faulkner chapters a couple months later sowed a seed of doubt amongst the colleagues about whether they actually had my number. Could Jack Shock be a comer? A distinguished visitor from Yale who requested my company for lunch, a second invitation to give a lecture, this time in New Haven, on Robert Johnson — which I brilliantly declined, mostly because I was too hung over to plan the trip — all these things worked like Ahab's subterranean miner to erode the department's certainty that I was a loser, plain and simple. I never got wind of any of the undercurrents, locked in my bourbon-bemused solipsism of work and drink, but Bill Smalls, more sensitive to the winds of change, probably did. A subtle estrangement grew between us. And into that estrangement walked Donna, with all the subtlety of a train wreck.

Donna, by transferring her attentions to Bill, derailed him. A man who would leave his adorable wife and kids for a siren like Donna — could such a man be serious? *Serious* or *not serious* were departmental code words for worth keeping and expendable. Pretty soon, my getting rid of Donna started to look like ruthlessness, a cardinal virtue in departmental eyes.

Looking back, I guess I owe what success I've scored in academic life to Donna and to Robert Johnson. Because if she hadn't fucked Mr. Ponytail in our kitchen, I probably would have clung to her like a rotten life preserver in a sea of marital battery acid. Though objectivity should have told me that losing her was like winning the lottery, Donna, so I told myself, was all I had, and without her life had ended for good and all. That last sentence, pathetic and melodramatic though it is, understates how I felt.

My debt to Robert Johnson was not paid by the book I wrote on him. I had long loved the descending phrase, the flattened third of the pentatonic scale. When I first picked up a guitar it was to bend a note. When I began to get good enough, I played the old country blues, mixing meters according to the feeling the music gave me. I learned my licks from old records by the masters: from Lightning Hopkins with his clean level Texas boogie and startling solos; from Big Bill Broonzy who could play better than the best in about any style he wanted — New Orleans, Delta, Texas, or Chicago; from Leadbelly with his sweet, high tenor and the interlocking of the baseline of his old Stella twelve string with his heeltaps; from Blind Willie McTell, another twelve string man, with his thin, plaintive wail and trembling rich vibrato; from Tampa Red, whose creamy slide always hit the note dead in the middle; from Blind Lemon, the father of them all, inimitable, with a way of making his guitar sound like an old piano, except that he could play it faster than any pianist, the notes falling in cascades like leaves driven before the wind; from Son House, with his stark, jangling slide and window-shaking baritone; from Scrapper Blackwell with his tremolo National, hell on bends and stays; from Scrapper's main man, Leroy Carr, whose songs I loved, full of irony and self-deprecation and despair; from Champion Jack, whose New Orleans piano blended diminished chords and stride. And most of all, from the haunted voice of Robert Johnson.

I remember the first time I heard that voice. I was at a party, and I had just taken a hit of reefer. The song was "Kind Hearted Woman."

Ain't but the one thing make Mr. Johnson drink . . .

Whenever that see you baby I begin to think.

Ooo baby, my life won't be the same . . .

The counterpoint of voice and guitar, both distorting sound, the voice like a record slowing down, and the triplet A chord on the seventh fret . . . And then soaring above it came that eerie falsetto "Oo, baby, my life won't be the same," the sound rising above the forlorn desire of the words themselves. Years later when someone found the photographs, I was drawn to the one in which Robert Johnson sits with the big Gibson Kalamazoo in his lap, a lit cigarette in his mouth. The face asymmetrical, one eye bulging, the other in a squint. The fingers preternaturally long and simian. The hair cut close to the head and the left ear bent forward a little like the handle of a sugar bowl. A man who looks more than a little drunk and who wears his guitar like an undershirt.

Why did I identify with a black man whose world I could know only in books and records? Maybe it was the car wreck that orphaned me as completely as if my father had died in it too. Or the sick in me that attracted me to a woman like Donna Gordon Prileau. And there was a night when I believed I met the demon himself. Driving drunk and stoned on a country road, I saw on the road in front of me a man, palm uplifted, grinning. With a squeal of brakes, my car spun over the bank into space, landing in the soft mud of a newly plowed field. In the silence that followed, Robert Johnson's voice screamed through the car speaker "Me and the Devil went walking side by side." Then the man walked to the bank, looked down at me. His face was black, scarred, the left eye almost closed in a squint. He was smoking a cigarette, clenched between gold-capped front teeth. "You and the Devil? White boy, you done seen the devil tonight." He laughed and when he walked away, his heeltaps echoed long in the still night, keeping syncopated time to the demon's song.

Maybe I'd have been the Jack Shock I am no matter what. Maybe, as the wizards of the science palace say, I am just an outcome of random chemicals acting on genotypes. Fated by genes to be thus and tempered here and there by events in the continuum of the wide Sargasso Sea. Pardon me if I prefer the demon theory. Throw into the mix the cannibal heart of Jack Shock that devoured what it loved. It was that heart that scared me now. That somehow by loving Sam I'd devour her too. Like the Robert Johnson who sang "I mistreated my baby and I don't know the reason why."

I lay in bed that night next to Sam thinking about the raveled threads of my life trying to discern the pattern in the carpet, except I couldn't picture the carpet, let alone the pattern, just the ravelings, like raw wool, clumped and scattered. I would say a word aloud, say love and listen to the sound of it disappear in the rhythm of her breathing. As much good as I felt for her, there was still the fear that it would leave me, like those heeltaps down a moonlit country lane.

I decided that I would lose her forever if she waked and saw me watching over her like that, like hell's own doorman opening wide the gates of abandon all hope. But she slept on.

I went upstairs to my own room and fell asleep. Around dawn I got up. I left a note on Sam's nightstand: I love you, it said. Be back for you soon if all goes well. Jack. I packed my bag in silence. I came down and stood at the threshold of that room which to me at that moment contained the sum of all the goodness and beauty that I had ever known and ever would know, and I turned and walked out of the house and got into the Continental, and beneath the oyster colored skies of the city morning, headed south towards Charlottesville.

7. A man is like a prisoner

A man is like a prisoner
He just can't be satisfied
Robert Johnson

MacGregor Hall, or as Bill liked to call it, the House of the Dead, is a vast, mostly windowless box resembling only vaguely the Greek revival academic buildings surrounding it, themselves copies of the founder's originals. It reminded me of a California mausoleum. Trudging down the hall on sepia colored linoleum, I made straight for Vandillingham's office. A copy of *Chronos,* the magazine he edited, was splayed like a dried bat in a glass box beside his office. The title of the lead article "Female Secretions in Proust" implanted itself in my mind with joyless insistence. A few steps more and I stood before the open door of the department chairman himself, hard at work at his desk, my loathing for him undimmed by two years of separation and no longer adulterated by the fear he had inspired before tenure dressed me in its cloak of invulnerability. Bernie was rich in hateables. For example, I'd forgotten how much I disliked his looks. He still affected a goatee and a wavy helmet of hair so clumpy and unnaturally dark that you wondered whether it was real or something he glued on. Then there was the part of him between goatee and hair. In my experience of it, Vandillingham's face wore just two expressions: a Gestapo sneer and a glacial stare of clinical inquiry. As I watched him recognize me, the frozen look gave way to the sneer. Good old Bernie, Mr. Reliable. I knocked and without waiting, walked in. Vandillingham looked up and shifted his glazed eyes about five degrees to the left of my face, another charming habit he had cultivated as a grace note in his affect. Vandillingham's academic youth had been dedicated to a biography of Pope. Now in the late middle of his life you saw Pope's venom but none of his humanity. When I last had known him, Vandillingham had taken up a vaguely continental lingo, a grasp at trendiness, and a sure sign of intellectual rigor mortis.

He symbolized everything I loathed about academic life: the passionless dogma, the arrogance, the contempt for what he taught. Did he like even Pope? Who could tell? I had gathered from listening to his lectures and from his comments in departmental functions that following the post-modern enthusiasts whom he cited as if they had the authority of Pope himself, he held the view that literature was irrelevant. *Moby Dick* was of no more value in his canon than a Mike Marvel comic book. During his time as chair of the department there had been a steady rise in the number of hires whose hair-splitting diatribes were completely impenetrable to anyone except — perhaps

43

— themselves and a tiny group of their ilk who had read the canon, some of whom professed to believe that words had no meaning anyway.

They were a grim lot, suffering from a peculiar exalted melancholia. There were no values and no meanings. As far as I could tell this desert included everything except the oases of their own brilliance. Someday somebody was going to gavel down the whole pretentious business. The talking heads of academia would start speaking English again. Until then the real books would have to survive because they were worth your time. People would read them because they needed to believe, as Vandillingham might say, that subjective variables like truth and beauty did exist.

"Shock," he said, and added superfluously and with real dismay, "You've come back."

I nodded.

Wordlessly he passed me a copy of the schedule of my teaching assignments. He had bent his head down over his desk and I found myself staring down his toupee, if that's what it was, shellacked to perfection. I glanced over my assignments. He had me down for the Twentieth Century Survey and a graduate seminar in Southern Literature. I was surprised that apparently he had nothing punitive in store for me. I turned to go.

"Just a minute Shock."

I turned again and faced his toupee.

"Beautiful head of hair you've got" I said.

He raised his face to mine. There was a touch of incredulity in the sneer that greeted my remark.

"We're not here to talk about my appearance, Shock."

"No," I agreed.

"No. We're going to talk about you. About your last semester here."

"Whatever," I said. So far I was enjoying myself.

"Your wife — "

"Ex-wife." I cut in.

"I believe not." He gave me now a full dose of the sneer. I remembered with a sudden hollow feeling that Leo McCardell had said the same thing. Donna, God bless her tiny heart, was quite capable of not having filed the divorce decree I had signed. Moreover, such a lapse was likely to be premeditated and was completely in character, power over something male, being Donna's ambrosia.

"My wife what?"

"Your wife alleges an affair between you and one of your students."

"A female?" I asked, deadpan. He nodded.

"Lucky girl," I answered. "Who was she?"

"None of your cheek, Shock."

"None of your pseudo-Brit argot, Vandillingham. Where are you from, anyway? Idaho, isn't it?"

"Spare me your red herrings, Shock."

He luxuriated in his advantage, basting me with the clinical look.

"Beautiful head of herrings you've got," I said. "Who, by the way, is she?" There ensued a long silence as Vandillingham sought to regain the meridian of his bipolar affect.

"*She* is Susan Monteith."

"Yeah?" I kept a poker face.

"You were sleeping with her."

"Says who? Susan Monteith? or Donna?"

"Donna — your wife." The mention of Donna and wife in the same sentence set me off again.

"Fuck Donna, Vandillingham." Everyone else has, I thought. "Why don't you drag *her* in here for the third degree?" I didn't really know the precise number of my colleagues, friends, enemies, and none-of-the-aboves to whom Donna had yielded up the fruit of her womanhood. But I was certain Vandillingham had not been one of them, his own taste running to pretty boys with surfer looks and surfer souls.

"That's another matter entirely."

"What exactly does Susan Monteith say about all this?"

"She has said nothing."

"In other words, Vandillingham," I was getting a lot of mileage out of the consonants in the chairman's name, and it gave me some pleasure to see that I was getting to him. "You're just busting my balls over some innuendo dropped by my ex — you say not — wife, while in fact Susan Monteith hasn't alleged a thing. Give me a break!" I waited. "Anything else?" "Good," I said when silence and the sneer met my question. "I'm going to the Ombudsman's office to file a complaint."

Cocky as Colonel Blimp, I turned and swaggered down the hall. Unlike Colonel Blimp though, I had in fact slept with Susan Monteith, though not while she was my student. I'd have gone off to my office except I didn't know where my new office was, if I still actually had one. I wasn't up to a reunion with the department secretaries and I was certainly not going to the Ombudsman. Sleeping with undergraduates, as that pseudo-limey Vandillingham might say, was a rum show at the University. I walked outside and lit up a cigarette and sat down on the step. The vista was deserted and oddly peaceful. Donna, you little bitch, I was thinking. Where in hell are you? Am I still married to you? If so, why? How many years would they give me for matrimonial axe murder?

The answer to the first of my questions I reflected was probably about three feet away in the pay phone just inside the door. First I tried Rucker who was out of town, damn him. A minute later I was talking to the substitute receptionist for Sally Hemming's Realty, Donna's oh-so-chi-chi firm, catering exclusively — but not really — to women clients. Hazel, the usual receptionist, was out for the day. Luckily, my voice was as unfamiliar to the temp receptionist as hers was to me.

"May I please speak to Donna Shock?"

"May I tell her who's calling?"

"It's a surprise."

A second later I heard Donna's contralto.

"Hello."

"Donna, you lovely piece," I said into the phone. "Can you meet me for a nooner?" There was a pause.

"Jack," she said. When I heard her smoky voice, I had to admit, for all I hated her guts, the sound of it tingled down my root bones.

"Why of course, sugar," she said. "Why else did I marry you?"

"Actually, I was hoping we were divorced."

There was a pause. "We should talk." This was Donna's standard line whenever she had a speech to make. And you could bet that insincerity and naked self-interest would be at the heart of it. I thought it wise to play Donna's game until I could see the lie of the land.

"How about lunch?"

"Dinner would be better."

"Better for what?"

"For everything. Fellini's," she said and hung up.

Fellini's is an old post-and-beam brick house just off the downtown mall converted into a bar and restaurant. Its decor is a tribute to the Italian director. The old movie posters that accompany the tables give them their names — "Dolce" for *La Dolce Vita*, and so forth. It was the bar where I was chaired before I was tenured, where by the third year of my assistant professorship I spent whatever time I had left over from the blues-and-Faulkner book boosting my amateur status as boozer and rakehell. And the bar where I'd gotten to know Susan Monteith.

46

As my marriage was disintegrating, I started playing my Old National Steel in various bars under the pseudonym Byron Nemo. My venues were at various dives around the mall and for dinner and drinks and very little money. After Bill left Betsey for Donna, music led me straight into the arms of Susan who waited tables at Fellini's the nights that I played there. She looked great and smiled a lot, wearing a short, short dress that showed off her plump calves. One night around graduation I found myself upstairs after hours with those calves up over my shoulders as I plowed her garden in the street-lit room. After that we met at her place. Susan had a picture of that grubby Irish actor from *9 1/2 Weeks* over her bed and though I've never seen the movie and look nothing like the man in the poster, she had me type cast. For the last year of my untenured life at the University, I was the poster boy's faithful understudy, though not the only one.

Susan's real boyfriend was the long-suffering kind. I knew about him from the start but he always seemed more theoretical than real, probably because he lived in Richmond. Susan visited him only on Tuesdays, one of the days I set aside for work. I don't know what he thought of me, poor bastard, but I pitied him for putting up with it. Susan's way of justifying sleeping with me was that she thought she loved me. She said she slept with her boyfriend because she knew he loved her. Our triangle was a tale of post-modern love with the motto: Have your cake and eat it too. I stayed with her for a summer although I didn't kid myself about the durability of our passion because I was so damn lonely, and for all her double heart she was a sweet thing too.

One August night on my way up Water Street I saw Susan sitting in a car talking to the Rival as I jeeringly referred to him. I don't know how I knew it was him, but who else could it have been, the way he was looking at her? They were so wrapped up in each other, they never noticed me. I was standing just inside a storefront to get out of a steady rain that had slicked down the streets. Susan and I were to meet in an hour even though it was a Tuesday night. I guess the Rival had driven down to Charlottesville to see her anyway. He was holding her hand and crying quietly, not even talking, just looking in her eyes while the tears fell from his own. She touched his cheek. He tried to kiss her but she turned her head aside a little. Then she got out of the car and ran down the street in the rain towards Fellini's.

He sat there for a while in his car. Then he looked up and saw me watching him. I don't know how he knew me, but he must have. He looked like he'd just been kicked in the guts. He dropped his head and reached for something. Melodramatically, I thought it might be a gun. It was just his keys. It took him a while to get it in, his hand was shaking that much. You poor bastard, I said to no one. And I thought I had it bad. He drove off very slowly, like a drunk trying to pretend he's sober as he comes up on a road block. It didn't occur to me then how much we were alike, with our half loves. About a week after seeing the Rival, I broke it off with Susan for the first time, though it was another six weeks before I could make it stick. It wasn't easy. I think she thought she was telling the truth when she said she was in love with me. I know I had it pretty bad for her, but I didn't love her like the other guy did. I didn't love anyone like he loved her, not then.

It was about three o'clock. I'd spent the day since my interview with Vandillingham visiting various university bureaucracies trying to get my pay started up again. Finally, I walked back to McGregor Hall, one of many ants streaming back to the ant farm. The secretarial pool in the front office didn't look familiar, but one of them pointed me towards a cardboard box the size of a television containing two years of mail and a key to my new office. Despite tenure, it was just another windowless crypt in the House of the Dead.

As I walked into the graduate student lounge in search of some bad coffee, I eavesdropped unwillingly on a conversation between a Chinese feminist and a Doctor Strangelove clone, who were arguing over what some tongue-thickening diatribist of the moment had really meant by something or other. Lots of luck I thought. I got depressed by the sheer ignorance of the PhDs that were being cranked out by the Department of English. So few of them had read any literature. Had any of them read the *Iliad* or *Don Quixote* or *Vanity Fair* or *Middlemarch* or *Leaves of Grass?* Too often the answer would be no one. I mean no one. And unless they had one of those unfashionable courses in great books as an undergraduate, they weren't going to either. Certainly not in the House of the Dead. For their dissertations they staked out some victim they didn't really care much about anyway and saturated their minds with his or her opus and then piled on some post-modernist politically correct jargon. I had read some of these tomes, unfortunately. Deader English you wouldn't care to know. I left the latest addition to the Great Debate in mid flow and mounted the stairs to my new crypt, lukewarm coffee in hand.

Unlocking the door, I sat down at a pseudo wood desk exactly like the one I'd left behind two years before. It was as if I had never left. I decided to call Sam. There was a delay because the call was long distance and the university operator had to verify my I.D. number — the one the university had just given me in perpetuity, or for as long as tenure lasts any way. While I was waiting I began rummaging through the stack of mail the secretary had saved for me. About six inches into the top bundle, I noticed a familiar hand. The General's. I tore the envelope open. What lay on the page before me was stark and succinct.

Dear Jack,

After your mother died your Aunt Grace and I grew close for a time. Sam, your cousin, is actually your half-sister. You may treat this intelligence in any way you see fit. Knowing your affection for Sam, I have the fullest confidence in your probity as regards this matter.

Affectionately,

Your father,

J.S. Shock Sr., Brig. Gen. U.S.A.F.

I was staring at the letter when Sam's voice, fuzzy but unmistakable, spoke in my ear.

"Jack, is that you?"

It was a moment before I could bring myself to speak.

"Sam." I said.

"Jack?" And then, "What's wrong?"

I tried to speak. I felt emptied out.

"Look. Don't worry" I said unconvincingly. "I'll call you back."

"Jack, what is it?"

"It's a letter from ... I ... Look, I'll call you back tonight."

"Aren't you coming home?"

"No, I'll go out to the cabin."

"Call me."

"I will."

"I love you, Jackie."

"I know. Love you, baby."

"Love you, baby." And mercifully she hung up.

I don't know how I kept my voice together in that last interchange but somehow I did. I felt nauseated, like I'd been punched in the gut. I hated my old man so much at that moment that I'd have killed him again if he walked in the door. Bastard, I kept saying aloud. Bastard. Bastard. Bastard. Bastard. Then I started in on Motherfucker. I hadn't quite run out of epithets when an angry knock roused me.

"Yeah." I said.

"I'm trying to work next door," said a voice that I couldn't connect with age or sex.

"Yeah?"

"Could you hold it down."

"I'm composing poetry," I shouted. "So fuck off, asshole."

Jack Shock, Doctor of Philosophy in English. Back in the saddle again.

An hour later, I found myself walking — it felt more like staggering — down the Lawn between Cabell Hall and the Rotunda. There was a cold

January rain, ice beginning to form at my feet. It was about five o'clock and illogically enough I'd decided to walk the two miles to Fellini's.

8. Dust My Broom

I don't want no woman

wants every downtown man she meets.

Robert Johnson

You don't want to be caught walking West Main after dark; the hard livers come out of Dice Street and the Hardy Drive projects looking to headline the police blotters. But no one bothered me that night. Maybe it was my clothes that advertised to the local hell raisers that I had nothing to lose. Nahumpoc. I was wearing the same ragged flight jacket and old jeans that I'd worn that day after my old man died. Maybe it was my look. I felt like the walking dead. Every time I thought of Sam I would shudder with pain and say, whether aloud or in my head I wasn't clear: No - No - No - No - No. That's how I covered those two miles of sleeting rain. I was wet and cold when I walked through the doors of Fellini's. Behind the bar looking like a thirties movie star was Mick Reardon, a boon companion from the old days.

"Well, look who the rain drove in. Fucking A. Jack. Jack Shock. Where in hell have you been?"

"Guatemala, Mick." We shook hands.

Guatefuckingmala, land of the Mayas. "God you're brown, Jack. You look like Pancho Villa. Or the Frito Bandito."

Mick was looking pretty much like himself, a ruddy Irishman with a pigeon chest, a Barrymore profile, and a Melvyn Douglas moustache.

I looked past him to the soldierly array of bottles that lined the mirror behind the bar. "I need a belt, Mick."

"What'll it be, Jack? Wait, don't tell me. Jim Beam. Three shots shaken with ice and poured neat."

I nodded. "But make it five," I said.

"You got it."

Mick had a way of bobbing while he talked like a fit horse who likes his work. Watching him could make you tired. His accent was pure Baltimore: Power mower came out paramour. We had met years ago when Donna had given me a big broken-down bay gelding from Laurel named Autopilot that I'd moved out to my pastures at the cabin. It turned out Mick had once bet on that horse. I'll bet he knew more about its track record than the trainer did. He was writing a book — it was probably behind the bar at that very minute —

that showed how you too could bet your way to a fortune, although Mick never had.

"What were you doing down there, Jack? You and Fay Wray run into trouble with the big monkey?"

"Just the usual, Mick." I watched him making the drink; it seemed to take a long time.

Mick set the glass in front of me and next to it a glass of ice water. I took a sip of the water first to wet my throat and then I drank the five shots, closer to six with Mick pouring them, in one galloping belt. I could feel the bender coming on. It was a physical sensation, a tremor in the hands, a tightness in the chest that made my voice quaver when I spoke. My mind kept running. Anything to keep from thinking.

"Seen Susan?" Mick had spread his hands out along the bar and was resting his weight on it. "I hear she's working at Whitey's"

"I just got into town."

"You know Donna's coming in tonight. She called for a reservation."

"I'm meeting her for dinner."

"You two aren't getting back together?"

"Not this side of paradise."

"She's no angel. Maybe a fallen one. She used to come in here a lot with some guy with an earring and a ponytail. Got one of those names that sound like the first half of a law firm."

"Dabney."

"Right. Beautiful woman."

"Skin deep."

Mick smiled and nodded.

"Will there be blood on the floor, or just tears?"

"Her tears, my blood." I tapped my glass on the bar. "Set me up again," I said. "Two more just like the first one."

Mick looked at me with mild incredulity. "Something wrong, Jack?"

"You wouldn't want to know." I nodded towards the bar. "Set me up again, Mick. Some Dutch courage and a pack of Camel shorts."

He set the pack down first and one after another two glasses of whiskey. A large party of people Mick knew came in, and he took them into the next room. I finished the first glass. Another group came in and the bar filled up. I could feel the whiskey working. I got up, and went over to contemplate my navel at the table Donna had reserved. Then I caught a glimpse of a familiar coiffure, too perfect to be real. Vandillingham was seated

52

at a far table, his head buried between the covers of *Chronos*. Something about the supercilious arrogance with which he greeted the world and the image of him reading that postmodernist rag he edited began to work on me, along with the bourbon and the rage I'd felt since reading the letter.

I noticed that nasty Vandillingham was surreptitiously scratching his balls. Certainly I had done such a thing myself from time to time, but I had a sudden, anti-postmodernist urge to ascribe meaning to his ball scratching.

"Something wrong with your balls tonight, Bernardo?" I yelled at him.

Vandillingham who so far had pointedly ignored me raised his face and glared at me, eyes full of malice.

"Shock," he said. "Well, well, well." Then he buried his face again between the covers of *Chronos,* and the consolation of female secretions.

Going after Vandillingham was clearly unwise. As chair of the department, he could make life very unpleasant for me. But the devil and Jim Beam were in me that night. I was about to give it to him with both barrels when the door opened. The first person through it was a tall blue-eyed male with a skier's tan and a head of gauzy sun-bleached California blonde hair. From behind me Vandillingham's voice called out in a positively syrupy greeting.

"Reg!"

I looked at Vandillingham. He was waving theatrically, his goat-like face suffused with hope. Then I felt a prickling down my neck. It was as if I could smell her. I turned. Standing behind Reg in a tight short black leather skirt and a tight black top, her breasts erect from the cold was Donna.

"Jack," she said. "God, you're tan." She took a drag on her cigarette. "Black."

She came over to the table and stood before me, smiling her crooked sharky little smile. Not as black as your heart I thought. "Donna," I said, my voice even. "A man would have to be crazy to divorce a woman looked as good as you."

She liked that, of course. It accorded well with her sense of herself as Donna Prileau, mover and shaker, consort of the cool, tasteful spender of daddy's money. But what she loved best was to be told she was still a sex kitten. That men wanted her just for her face and body. That she still had what it took. And God knows I wasn't flattering her. She did have what it took and probably would for a good long time. Lovely skin, covering that good tight body. Features that would last a while yet: a small aquiline nose, high cheekbones, a full well-shaped mouth. Only the eyes betrayed her; they were shrewd, knowing and hard. They held a warning for the initiated. No quarter asked or given. Her smile went a long way toward masking those predatory eyes; she used it, as she was using it now to charm, to assure you that you were the one she had come here for. That you too had what it took. You'd have thought that after all the different ways she had fucked me, literally and figuratively, that some sense of irony, if not of shame, would have kept that smile off her face. But no, she believed, I guess, that I was still dumb or sick or horny enough to lay aside all there had been between us and jump her bones again. Or maybe she was just glad to see me. Dear Jack, how can I jerk his chain one more time? You could almost see the wheels turning.

"How's your father?" she asked.

"He's dead."

She sat down across from me and covered my hand with her own, plump, strong, scarlet-tipped. There was a squeeze of reassurance.

"When?"

"Last week." It was at the tip of my tongue to add "as if you gave a damn." Because she didn't, I knew. There was no love lost between my father and Donna. They had sized each other up early on. His sangfroid had no appeal for her; neither was her frank sensuality his dish of tea.

"I'm so sorry, Jack."

"Me too."

"Has it been tough? I'm sorry, of course it has. It's just that I know you were never close to him."

"Close enough, it seems," I said.

"You look beaten. Sad, I mean. Poor baby."

She was overdoing it now. And when she reached out and caressed my cheek, it was not a gesture of consolation so much as a practiced use of friction, one of Donna's long suits. I thought about biting that hand; instead, mindful that she might still have some obscure power over my future, I said something that played into her scenario for the evening.

"Thanks. It's good to see a face from the old days."

Right now her face was wearing the expression of the abandoned wife who still loves her man enough to forget the past, and who chooses to stand by him in his hour of need.

I *was* suffering of course, but not because the old man was dead, although maybe that was part of it. It was Sam's face that flooded my mind. I tried not to think. Donna scanned me with her shrewd eyes: her next question seemed preternatural.

"How's Sam?"

"She's fine," I said.

"In love?" she asked.

"She's got some lawyer."

"Not the one that looks a little like you?"

"I didn't notice," I lied.

"He bought the cabin back for you, that lawyer — if I had known . . ." Donna must have realized that she was better off not completing this sentence. If she had known, well, she would have refused to sell the land to Charley-Boy, my father's agent. Or she'd have hiked the price up so high as to make the purchase impossible. I played dumb.

"I haven't been to see it yet," I said. Which was true.

"Where are you staying?" The pressure on my hand increased slightly. Good old Donna, a romp in the hay would do so much for her complexion.

"Not sure," I said.

"You can stay at my place." And I know exactly what's in store for me, I thought. I changed the subject.

"How's old Bill?"

"He and Betsey are trying to work things out. He's still looking for a job. It's his last semester." Donna's eyes and voice struggled for that note of sincere, though merely friendly, interest that no doubt she also had employed when speaking to Bill of me. Poor Jack. So lost. So confused.

"Betsey's a lot better woman than Bill deserves," I said.

"*You* always thought so. She's been seeing some Pakistani doctor — "

If Donna was about to justify sleeping with Bill by retailing some gossip about Betsey, I declined the gambit.

"Donna, my angel," I said, breaking in and broaching the matter closest to my own interest. "Are we divorced or still married?" She took a drag on her cigarette and let the smoke stream slowly between us. Then she smiled.

"Married."

"Ahhh. . ." I said putting as little as I could into the monosyllable.

"Those papers I signed ... the divorce decree?"

"I never filed them."

"Why?"

"Jack," she said, "you know you're the only man I've ever really loved." The pressure and the friction on my hand increased. Dear Donna. So consistent. Such a liar. She smiled.

"I miss fucking you." At this I laughed in spite of all my resolve to keep on Donna's good side, finding it difficult to believe that my cock and whatever went with it could have meant anything more to Donna than she could have found with any male of suitable dimensions, constancy being a very tiny star in the constellation of Donna's standards of marital conduct.

"Jack," she said taking an aggrieved tone, "you're mean." This little girl stuff she could see had no effect on me. She went on. "We've been everything to each other." Everything, I thought, but husband and wife. Donna's remark had probably come from yesterday's soap opera and had about as much to do with our years together as the sonnet "Let me not to the marriage of true minds admit impediments."

"How's the beamer?" I asked changing the subject, though I was pretty sure that Donna's car meant at least as much to her as I did.

"Fine," she said.

"Paint holding up?"

"You were really angry that day." She took a last drag and stabbed her cigarette out.

"Yes, I was."

"Poor Dabney," she said using her naughty girl voice, "It took him a whole year to grow his ponytail back."

"Good old Dabs," I said. "Teach him to pork another man's wife on the husband's kitchen counter."

"You were never home, Jack; we hardly ever saw each other, and when we did, all you wanted was a quickie to take the edge off."

"I never heard you complain. And nobody was ever slow enough or long enough for you, Donna dearest."

"You weren't."

"What about Bill Smalls. Did he live up to his name?"

Donna laughed. Her voice held a theatrically bitter note. She pulled another cigarette out and lit it.

"Same old Jack."

"Same old Donna."

She was smiling again, bravely through crocodile tears.

"You were the only one I ever really wanted to come home to."

"Like I came home to you and Mister Ponytail?"

"You know what I mean, Jack. I love you."

She looked at me with those beautiful, insincere, slightly askew green eyes. This was the moment Donna had been leading up to. I saw it now. I love you, Jack. Maybe she believed it too. For now. I'd seen this movie before. I remembered it from the time we'd split up when I was in graduate school and,

56

hey, after almost twelve years with me, Donna certainly had my number. I was one of those wounded incomplete men whose loneliness had a metaphysical slant to it, poor stupid bastard. I'd burnt my share of candles at Donna's altar over the years. Too many. I'd been naïve enough to believe her before. I'd been sick enough to need the kind of sexual arousal that depends on seeing yourself as essentially unlovable, pathetic enough to stay with this spoiled brat of a wife because I bought into her little rituals of control and gratification. And hell, who knows how sick anybody else's sex life is? Who knows whether what Donna and I had had was any sicker than what bounced the bedsprings of June and Ward after they put the Beaver and Wally to bed, or the couplings of Bernie Vandillingham and Reg the Surfer Boy. No, I didn't love Donna. I didn't love myself. I didn't love my old man. But I did love Sam. Right after Donna said I love you, Sam's face came into my head, and all the heart went out of me. I didn't want to play Donna's stupid little game of let's screw each other again, literally and figuratively, to see how much mileage we can get out of simple friction, illusion, lost youth, the consolation of a shared death wish — getting fancy now — which was about all we'd had together. But to tell the truth, I didn't want to hurt Donna either. My heart sank as I thought of Sam. I felt that I had always loved her. Would love her, wanted her even if all I had to offer her was misery. Maybe I'd never hold her in my arms again. If I had any kind of respect for the fundamental decencies, hell, for biology, I'd end it. I'd get on my buckskin and ride south to whatever oblivion of reeferdom would accept my passport and my money. But whatever I did, I was not going to fuck Donna again. That was dead. Dead as a hammer. No more winter dreams for Jack Shock of poor little rich girls with green eyes and yellow hair and pink BMW convertibles.

"Goodbye, Donna," I said standing up. "I've shot my bolt." And I went out the door.

9. A Drunken Hearted Man

I'm a drunken hearted man
and my life seems so misery.
Robert Johnson

As I walked out into the sleeting night, the wind knifing through my shirt, I thought of Sam and forced myself not to. I had intended to ask Donna for a ride back to my car. The going was icy and I didn't much cotton to the idea of another two-mile slog down Main Street to the University parking lot. Mick would have lent me his car, but I wasn't going back in for another scene of Donna's melodrama. The real melodrama was the one going on between my ears. "Sam," I said aloud in someone else's voice. I walked on muttering. "I'll get out of this." I said it over and over. "I'll get out of this."

Around the corner there were two or three bars where bottled solace might be for sale. Whitey's, a converted drugstore with a chessboard decor that looked like a set from *The Cabinet of Doctor Caligari* was the first door I came to. I had that feeling as I pushed my way in that I wanted to get to the bottom of a bottle of whatever bourbon they had most of. The place was crowded. The bartender on shift was Skipper Brown, a classmate of mine who had never gotten free of the night scene. I nodded to him and was making my way towards the bar through the crowd.

"Jack" I heard a woman's voice say behind me. I knew that voice.

Susan Monteith looked at me with gold-flecked green eyes. She had taken my hand and was squeezing it against her thigh.

"Can I buy you a drink?" she asked.

"You can buy me the bar," I said.

Smiling she half turned towards the back of the bar with a preoccupied look. I got the feeling she was afraid we were going to be interrupted. Behind her sat someone I recognized as a generic academic poet. He was gesturing scenically. I ignored him.

"Someone told me you'd left town, Susan."

"I did, but I'm back. Obviously."

"For how long?"

"Who knows? I'm working here, but not tonight."

I nodded. She was looking even better than the good she always looked. Susan always looked a little plumped up in the breasts and calves with ankles and wrists that tapered slenderly. She was a little taller than medium height and she wore her sheeny coppery-blond hair short in a pageboy fashion.

"How's the boyfriend?" I'd almost said the Rival.

"He's fine." She dropped her eyes. It was clear that nothing had changed. The Rival, poor bastard, was still waiting in the wings for whatever crumbs Susan tossed him on Tuesdays or weekends, or whatever their arrangement was these days. He was still whipped and she was still having her cake and eating it too. The fellow sitting at the table where she'd come from looked like the Rival's rival of the moment.

"I missed you, Jack."

"I've been hearing that a lot lately," I said graciously. I'm as susceptible to the muzak of the glands as the next poor bastard, as my knife-in-the-brain relationship with Donna shows. The old weakness for a girl with a beckoning eye. Weakness here being a better word than, say, longing. Susan and I had had our moment in the sun and we couldn't make it work. She was certainly a cut above Donna in the post modern MacDonald's of today's body exchange, if *nice* still counts for something. For all her incentives, let us call them, Susan had never fully lodged in my heart. She liked to tell me that I had found my way into hers. Who knows? Maybe hers wasn't the deepest heart, and maybe it was capable of duplicity, but it was still the part of herself she cherished, more than her very good mind which she used off-handedly, even contemptuously. With her brains another student might have won a full scholarship for the doctorate. For Susan academia was the house salad, not the bouillabaisse.

"I see you've found consolation in my absence." I nodded towards the poet. He was dressed all in black as had been the custom amongst self-advertising intellectuals when I'd left the country a couple of years before, and the look certainly suited him. Black shoes, black socks, black britches, black shirt, black sports coat. He looked like the undertaker's apprentice. He had that dead white, just-crawled-out-from-under-a-rock complexion that had been in vogue for a long time now. Except in his case, there was a pimple or two to spoil the effect. It was the same Anorexic-Junkie-Look that you saw in a lot of young women, as if at the very peak of their vitality they were trying to look as close to dead as they possibly could. Susan, God bless her genes, was biologically unsuited to the embalmed look. Her current boyfriend wore a ponytail and an earring too and a snooty my ass-weighs-a-ton look, none of which endeared him to me, although touches like these probably didn't hurt him with a certain kind of woman, neurotic, self-absorbed, and probably in thrall to intellectualized female secretions. He smoked ostentatiously, using a lot of spidery gestures. The sight of him poured Miracle Grow on my favorite prejudices; I was in a mood to trip him up if he came around me.

"Drew." Susan said matter of factly, following my gaze. "Do you want to meet him?"

"Not particularly."

"Uh oh. You look like you're suffering from a testosterone overdose."

"You might be right" I said, "He looks a lot like a guy I caught fucking my ex-wife one time."

"And what did you do?" She was giving me her frank look, the look that she used just before she used to lead me off to bed.

"Oh, we dialogued," I said.

"I'll bet."

I was about to bring up the details of my little chat with Vandillingham, when I looked at Drew and thought better of it. For all I know he was the first alternate in the Vandillingham pin-up contest. Besides, Susan was starting to ease into her mating dance. She'd kept hold of my hand all this time and now she took it in both of hers and hugged it between her breasts. Susan flirted and she was never half-hearted about it. I liked that about her. But every time I looked at her all I saw was Sam. Even so, I hated to see her with this oatmeal-faced poet manqué. Calm down, Jack, I was saying to myself. You came here to bury Caesar, or rather to drink him to death, not to lead him into battle.

Just then Drew spidered his way over and stood proprietarily behind Susan with his hands on her shoulders, leaning in. My hand was in Susan's; she held it between her breasts. God knows, we made an odd triptych.

"Hi," he said, smiling with everything but his eyes. "You're Jack."

"That I am," I said. "At least to my friends."

He ignored me.

"Weren't we going to that thing at Bill Smalls?" he half whispered conspiratorially in her ear. "We're already late."

Susan was staring at me. I believe I was at the stage of drunk where you smile a lot and turn pink. Susan took her lower lip between her teeth and winked at me.

"I'd like to go home," she said to me.

"But what about the Smalls thing," Drew said.

"You go without me."

"But you wanted to go."

She turned to face him. "I've got to talk to Jack," she said.

"I need a ride," I said helpfully. I really did need a ride of course, but that wasn't why I butted in. I liked the idea of Drew showing up late and without Susan at the Smalls thing. I liked the idea that it would come out that Susan had stayed behind with me and that this piece of intelligence would inevitably get back to Vandillingham who would use it as a pretext to get me into his office for a post modern intimidation session, whereupon I could tweak him with some reminiscence about dear Reg. My aspirations were mean-spirited, but in my present mood, what I longed for more than anything was an explosion, something to force me out of myself. So I clung disingenuously to Susan or more accurately, allowed her to cling to me.

Without a word Drew turned and strode out of Whitey's, the picture of injured dignity, although even this was more than I was prepared to give him credit for. A powerful thirst welled up inside me. I encircled her with my left arm and guided her towards the bar where smiling Skipper was already shaking up three shots of Maker's Mark.

"Long time no see, Jack."

"Ditto, Skipper," I said. We shook hands. But my eyes were on the bourbon.

I hoisted the glass and threw the whiskey down in one belt. "Hit me again," I said. Susan looked a little alarmed and Skipper shook his head.

"You driving, Jack?" he asked.

"No," I said. "She is."

Skipper, an ex-drunk, liked commenting on my ingestions. Probably because we were the same age and had shared a lot of habits good and bad over years, his hectoring never much bothered me. He was a real guitar man in the ripping Clapton style of the late sixties. He had a fair, freckled face, permanently startled pale blue eyes, and shoulders that sloped like a church roof. Eight years ago he had fronted the hottest band in town. As far as I knew he had been really in love only once with one of those crazy women with a streak of meanness musicians always get a shot at. Witness Donna dearest. It hadn't worked out. Not the band. Not the girl. So far he'd never shown any interest in a job that would have removed him from the night scene he had starred in until bad love and whiskey had put him on the floor. He was unembittered by failure, if failure was what his life to this point had been. Despite his comments on my drinking, he cared nothing for the world of quasi-respectability which I inhabited, though hardly an illustrious example. And I was glad that he seemed genuinely happy to see me and that he didn't seem especially curious about what I'd done or where I'd been the last two years, as if he'd taken it for granted all along that I'd return and resume my old life as effortlessly, at least in his eyes, as I had left it. That was one of the things I liked about the night scene in Charlottesville. In D.C. after a year or so on the road you wouldn't recognize any of the people you ran into in a place where you'd been a regular six months before.

Behind me the band had begun playing something that required about as much musical talent as operating a chain saw. The few chords played were loud and distorted through a Marshall Double Stack. The group's name, The

Thumbheads, described the collective appeal from the neck up of the band members. Their audience was composed mostly of rowdy young women dressed less to cover than to expose. The lead singer for the Thumbheads, and the most thumbheaded of the four, wore a tee shirt with a face painted on a thumb wearing the same wolfish smile as himself. He had a knobby complexion and a greasy, carefully messed up flat top and an obscure tattoo on his forearm. I gathered that the group was playing its theme song:

She's got every disease.
As she drops to her knees,
She's just dying to please.
But she's got every disease.

As insulting as these lyrics were to womankind, they inspired transports of passionate adulation among the crowd. Two neo-hippie deadheads were dancing barefoot in front of the band. One, a blond with long straw-colored hair, I distinctly remembered as a flaming feminist. I felt myself coming down with the post modern blues again.

Susan wasn't a Thumbhead fan, she assured me; she and the poet had been brooding together over Sambucca when the band kicked in. Yes, the Rival was still very much in the picture as a weekend love — the ponytailed poet had replaced me as the meat and potatoes of weekday fare.

"The more it changes, the more it stays the same," I said when Susan explained the arrangement. She threw me a hurt look that still managed to convey a certain sexual provocation.

"You mean us," she said.

"You're still very much yourself," I answered, "but he's not much like me. Maybe he's an improvement."

"I loved you, Jack."

"I remember," I said. "Hot stuff, but not mine alone."

"I never said it would be."

"You never said. Period."

"You knew."

"Yes, I knew. I kidded myself. I'm good at it." Drunk as I was, I felt pretentious as hell saying this.

"Maybe I want what you wanted too — now."

"Maybe," I said. Maybe not, I thought. Certainly not. Susan was one of those women about whom Wyatt had written "They flee from me that

62

sometime did me seek." All the while she lay in your arms, she was staring at the exit sign. She might settle down for a while at the end of her twenties but even then she'd keep a man on his toes. She wanted her share and then some, and she was good looking enough, and more importantly, willful enough to get what she wanted. Although I'd gotten what I wanted too, if I hadn't been a drunk in a bad marriage, I'd have never gone for it. Bourbon took the edge off anybody's sense of irony. Let's hear it for Susan and the brackish joys of love on the half shell — the kind that left an aftertaste like the wrong end of a dead cigarette.

She stood on her toes and kissed me. She was a good kisser. For a minute, a long minute, because undeniably she made my pants dance, I thought about the promise of that kiss. For the last two years it hadn't mattered whose arms I was in as long as the hydraulics worked. Even though I wasn't sober enough to pass scrutiny at a sobriety stop, I wasn't drunk enough to jump Susan's bones tonight. And doomed as love with Sam might be, I had to play that hand. I broke off the kiss.

"Let's go to my place," she said.

"Let's just go," I answered.

10. The Queen of Spades

She's a little Queen of Spades
Men will not let her be.

Robert Johnson

Walking arm and arm with Susan, I gazed at the world through bourbon-colored glasses. In my brilliant stupor, I noticed everything: cracks in the sidewalk bricks, galls on the willow oaks, empty newspaper vending boxes, dead flies at the feet of storefront manikins — all of it in my mind suffused with a Dylan Thomas splendor. "Fern Hill" comes to the Downtown Mall. Drunk, I felt safe. Sam and I were safe. I forgot about Susan, despite the fact she had my right arm gathered to her breast and as she stared into my eyes with pole axed ardor. Pacing me to her car, she opened my door and as I nestled into the seat, she bent her head and kissed me.

"Dear heart," she said, "how like you this?"

"Ah. Wyatt," I said, the post-modern version, I thought. She gave me a melting look and kissed me again.

I was drunk and Lord knows she looked good. I couldn't help smiling with her smile.

"Susan, I'm in love."

"So am I."

"Uh huh. But the girl I love is in Washington."

"Good. We're here."

"Not good."

She kissed me and lowlife that I am I kissed her back. And it went on like that. Her hand was in my lap and I was hard.

"Whoa ..." I said.

"Can't you just let me love you?"

"This girl ..." I said.

"Don't tell me about her."

"Susan . . ."

She had my cock in her hand and squeezed it through my britches.

"I want you inside me, Jack."

64

Just then a group of revelers rounded the corner and Susan stood up and looked down at me.

"You're not getting off that easily."

"I never do," I said. She went around, got in, leaned over and kissed my cheek.

"Where to then?" she asked.

I don't know what made me answer as I did because I certainly had nothing to gain by it, and a fair amount to lose.

"Bill Smalls' party," I said.

"Are you serious?"

"No, I'm drunk," I said. "And I'd like to share a little of the good cheer with my colleagues."

"They may not let you in."

"They'll let me in," I said. "They wouldn't miss it for the world."

Two corners down from the house where I had assaulted Donna's Beamer, stood Bill Smalls' house, light streaming from the windows. There was no music, just a hum of voices that gave way from time to time to excruciating laughter. After a couple of years of slumming in Central America, and the intensities of the last two weeks in Washington, not to mention The Letter From The Grave, it felt oddly comforting to knock at a door where galloping neuroses and battles of the ego were the worst I had to fear.

Bill himself came to answer my knock, the haggard joviality of his look belying the failure I knew he believed himself to be. The gods of MacGregor Hall had withheld their favor. Their judgement of him was now his of himself.

"Jack!" Shaking my hand while he gripped me by the shoulder, he seemed, against all odds, actually glad I'd come. "It's good to see you."

"You too," I said. Whiskey had made me sentimentally oblivious to certain blemishes on our friendship: a little matter of adultery with my wife, although adultery seemed altogether too exalted a term for sex with Donna.

"Come in," he said, theatrically gesturing to the suddenly silent room beyond.

Arrayed around him stood the post-modern politically correct aristocracy of the University, come to mourn the passing of one of their own. In the minds of many of them I was the son of a bitch of all too modest gifts who had knocked their fair-haired boy from his marble pedestal.

Slumped in the corner in a parody of seductive lassitude, Vandillingham was pouring his heart out to Reg the Surfer Boy. He glanced my way, a basilisk of malice. The muzak of the glands had him in its throes too and it was clear that he had no idea that the girl on my arm was the hot little twist, to put it in his pseudo Brit argot, whom I'd been wanking the summer before I left for the lesser Antilles. Conferring with them was Susan's new other boyfriend Drew, who pointedly ignored us both. Nearby was Tru Bart, the pop culture guru of the department, a stout, spotty, broad-faced woman with hair like a paint brush that has been badly cleaned. Her court consisted of three graduate students, two of whom I vaguely remembered as persons to dodge at all costs, one an androgyny whose hair flattered neither of the sexes to which he or she seemed simultaneously to lay claim. The other was a woman with a hyphenated name, both names being Eastern European and unpronounceable by me in the state I was in. With them was Dial Birdsong, a Mississippian with a taste for old music, and a gift for playing it. Seeing Dial reminded me that these last years I had been able to play the music I loved only in my head. Donna had pawned the '29 Duolian she had given me when we were first married. A twelve-fret round neck with a keening whine in its high ranges. Even-keeled Dial was smiling at something Tru had just said. With the physique of a young Alfred Hitchcock, Dial was also the only person in the room that I actually felt glad to see.

"Dial, God bless your heart," I called out to him. "Still got that old Gibson Banner?"

Dial turned, his face a study in stymied memory.

"Jack! By God, Jack, it's damn good to see you." He flashed a look at Susan and a half glance at Vandillingham and suddenly thought better of whatever he was going to say.

To his right a pretentious looking personage — as Henry James might have described him — took studied notice of my arrival. I absorbed his face with a glance, without pausing to consider him.

Behind me Bill Smalls was making happy squirting noises. Susan had kept hold of my arm, but hadn't said a word. Looking at her now, I admired her composure in this Olympian gathering of talking heads.

Bill Smalls was certainly very drunk. I had an idea, probably flattering to me, that he was even drunker than I. At the moment Bill was trying to get the room quiet by beating the air and pursing his lips. The clump of academics who nested with the self-important personage fell silent first. Bill shushed them with a gesture like a maestro stilling an adagio from the string section. Then he sought out Vandillingham and actually led him by the hand away from Reg, unaware of the bad smell look on the chairman's face.

"Everyone. Please," he said, "a moment of silence."

Bill had gotten the whole party into an amoeba-shaped lump in the center of his living room. The Dimitry Karamazov look on his face kept me on the balls of my feet. I wasn't the only member of that captive audience glancing longingly towards the door. More witnesses arrived from other rooms. Wilfred Lumbley, the Freudian-turned-New-Historicist strode past me in mid bellow, trailing Adrien Von Stein, the specialist in feminist studies, and Fontana Dupree, the Haitian polyculturalist. Bruno Kudra, an eighteenth-century cohort of Vandillingham, late of Johns Hopkins, headed a contingent from the kitchen; Alice Poulet (no relation to Georges), who had been trucked in from Yale to head the department's Women's Studies Program, was one of them. It seemed that the whole of PM, PC Charlottesville was standing in that circle, looking at me with as much compassion as a group of diners inspecting the star oinker at a pig roast.

"Friends, Romans, Colleagues," Bill began. He then laughed uproariously, or rather gave an unconvincing impersonation of a man laughing uproariously and flailing his arms. No one joined in.

"Lend me your ears."

At this, he inadvertently gave Vandillingham's hair a tug. I was happy but not surprised to see that it moved like a clump of moss, and that despite Vandillingham's indignant attempts to reposition it, it remained just enough askew to give him the look of a Yorkshire terrier who had been severely misgroomed. Once again Bill indulged in his parody of a laugh and once again, except for a snort from one of the kitchen crew, no one joined him, although the self-important personage grinned sadistically.

"I have something to say," he paused. Like a light house beacon he flashed his glazed stare at every corner of the room.

"Jack Shock, the best friend I ever had, has returned at last from beautiful Nicaragua."

In fact, Nicaragua was the one Central American country I hadn't visited, but I said nothing.

"His wonderful book on Robert Johnson has been given the Talliaferro Award."

This was news to me. I did vaguely remember a portentous looking envelope bearing some official-looking inscription, but I hadn't opened it or anything after I had read the General's letter. On the other hand it might very well be that Bill had simply gotten his facts wrong. Reliability was probably not his long suit just at the moment.

"Bill," I said. Though I was still drunk, I was sober enough to know that Bill was on the verge of a painful self-humiliation that he would find even more so in retrospect. I had no desire to be a part of it. He tottered towards me with Boris Karloff steps smiling a Boris Karloff smile. I felt his right arm go round my shoulder and then a pincer-like grip on the back of my neck; I felt like the mullet in the pelican's beak.

"Francophiles, Romanians and Collegians," Bill began, returning to his theme for the evening. He had the dead white pallor of a red-eyed passed-out-walking-drunk. As if convulsed with silent laughter, he hugged his chest with his free hand and ducked, but when he raised his face, anger gleamed in his blood-filled eyes.

"Next year I will not be among you. I don't know where I'll be. I don't know what I'll be. I don't know if I'll be. But you can take comfort in knowing that Jack Shock," I felt his hand clutch at my neck spasmodically, "will be here in all his black-and-blues splendor." He had begun to shout. "Congratulations, Jack." He loosed his hold on my neck long enough to pound me twice very hard on the back. I turned towards him, breaking his hold. I was feeling grim.

"Jack, despite his sunburned face, is a Caucasian. Blacked yourself up down in Niggeragua, didn't you, Jack? Did I say Niggeragua? Sorry, Jack. I meant Guatemala."

"Bill —"

"Oh, you are a deep one, Jackie," he broke in. "A deep one. Who'd have thought it? Old Jack, a white boy, tenured in an African-American position. Who's that buck you wrote about, Blind Lemon Pledge?" He was reaching for me again.

"Don't you touch me, Bill," I said.

"I'm going to teach you, Kernel," he said, coming at me with a Faulknerian haymaker.

It was a telegraphed punch. I ducked, taking Susan down with me. I watched Bill's punch land squarely on the nose, and it was a big one, of the Important Personage, who staggered backwards and sat down, bleeding from both nostrils.

"Let's move," I said to Susan. We scrambled, crabways on all fours towards the door. There we watched as the impact of his punch set Bill off on a jeremiad against his own icons.

"It's all fucking pointless, mother-fuckers!" Bill screamed, staring wildly at his guests.

"It's all lies. Read Foucault. There's no fucking point to any of it."

Like a diving beetle he lunged for Drew, who had been standing, smiling with studied imperturbability, nodding at Bill's every word. Bill had gotten Drew by the throat and he began shaking him so hard that Drew's ponytail came undone. His hair whipped wildly, like a black curtain caught by the wind, through which, now and then, you glimpsed his bulging eyes. Reg the Surfer Boy had taken hold of one of Bill's hands and was trying to pry it loose from Drew's throat. Gamely, Dial went for the other hand. Vandillingham was stuttering incoherently, spittle flying. He had grabbed his toupee and was pulling it from side to side like a scalp massager. One or two of the women and several of the men had begun to scream.

"Jack," Susan's whisper was almost a shout. "You've got to stop him; he'll kill Drew."

Actually I was enjoying myself immensely. What Bill was doing to Drew I had fantasized about doing myself when we were at Whitey's. What he had done to El Importante, I had enjoyed watching, the way you watch a cartoon. But what Bill had gotten Vandillingham to do to himself, now that was genius, however unintentional. "Read Derrida!" Bill was shouting. "Classical logic is dead, motherfucker! Read Lacan! Language is fucked, you pissants."

Susan was right, of course. Someone had to stop Bill, if only to keep him off death row. And since I was directly behind him, I had a chance to interfere with him in an undetected way. Over Bill's shoulder I could see that Drew's usual Maalox pallor had given way to reddish purple. Standing up directly behind Bill, I raised my heel and kicked hard against the inside of Bill's right knee. He went down instantly, turning Drew loose as he fell. Drew staggered gasping into the arms of Reg who began to perform ostentatious mouth-to-mouth resuscitation. Vandillingham took this medical infidelity rather hard, staring at Reg with the closest thing to a vulnerable expression I had ever seen on his face. Very sensibly Dial sat down on Bill's butt to immobilize him. Then Tru Bart joined him astride Bill's upper back, making at least four hundred and fifty pounds in all.

"Fuck you, Jack Shock," Bill was yelling, "you goddamned phony hairball piece of shit from hell."

The important-looking personage sat blubbering for all he was worth, blood, snot and tears falling from his face in clots, curds and drips. Susan sobbed quietly beside me on her knees. I got her up and guided her towards the door.

"Shock, you motherfucker —" was the last thing I heard as I pulled the door shut.

Susan and I sat down together on the stoop. She laid her head on my shoulder as I looked up at the stars.

"I'll give Bill one thing," I said. "No whimpering fare-you-well for him. It was bang-bang all the way."

"Jack," Susan had taken my hand and was looking into my eyes with that peculiar earnestness that she used even to ask me to pass the peanut butter.

"Susan." I squeezed her hand in return.

"I've got to go and see how Drew is."

"Right," I said.

"Are you angry?"

"At who? Drew?"

"At me."

"Nuh-uh. Go see how Drew is."

"Will you wait for me?"

"Darling, you are my eyes, ears and wheels tonight."

"I'll be right back."

"Take your time; I'm not in any hurry."

"I was hoping you were," Susan smiled and touched my face.

I watched Susan disappear through the door. It was a lot quieter now than when we'd come. The door opened suddenly sending a blast of light onto my face. El Importante, looking greatly chastened by the sock in the snout he had manfully taken in my stead, staggered out assisted by the androgyny and the hyphenated Eastern European woman. He looked at me with it-should-have-been-you eyes and staggered by. Ah well. Another potential bosom buddy in the department lost forever. Then Tru Bart lumbered out.

"God, Jack," she said. "Does trouble follow you or what? Where have you been anyway, Samoa?"

"Life is a beach, Tru."

"A bitch?"

"Tru, my angel, don't mind-fuck me, not tonight."

"She bent down and kissed me lightly on the cheek. I missed you Jack. You play the best slide guitar in MacGregor Hall."

"Damned with faint praise, Tru."

"Jack, watch your back. Bernie is out for your blood."

"He can have it."

"He just found out that you came to the party with Susan Monteith."

"The victim of my satanic lusts?" Speak of the devil, the victim herself emerged trailing Drew, newly risen from the dead, not that he looked any more alive, or dead for that matter, than before.

"Susan, I need you," he said hoarsely.

"Drew ..." Susan took a step towards me.

"Hey Drew," I said, smiling, "I guess you owe me your life."

The look Drew threw in my direction fell considerably short of gratitude.

"Next time, I'll let Bill send you on down the line," I said.

Drew had taken Susan aside and was importuning her with the pathos of his near-death experience, which had the storied effect of stoking the fires of his libido. Judging by Susan's reaction, it didn't look like Drew was going to get any booty tonight. Not that I was planning on laying any pipe in Susan's

70

well either. I got up, retreated to a discreet shrub with a view of the road and sky and lit up a cigarette, wishing it were reefer. Before it got icy, the rain had slicked the streets down tarry black. A sliver of moon knifed through the clouds like a trout breasting the current. It was not the worst moment of the day. Not by a long sight.

11. Stop Breaking Down

Every time I go out on the street

Some pretty momma start breaking down on me.

Robert Johnson

I was leaning against a street lamp communing with a patch of stars. The moon lay hidden now in a cloud bank toward the east. A woman's voice rang shrill, "Fore!" From behind the shadow of a boxwood a cigarette came sailing and hit me squarely between the eyes. Smoke came streaming from the shadows towards the light. Footsteps. Donna's face.

"Fore, Donna? Or foreplay?"

"You wish."

I touched my forehead. There was a raw spot there where a piece of burning glop had stuck for an instant, right about where they used to get you on Ash Wednesday. Burning, I felt like smoking. I reached for the pack of Camels in my shirt pocket. They were about half gone and a book of matches was still tucked inside the cellophane. I shook out a cigarette and lit it. I watched Donna over the cupped match, clouds of smoke still streaming from her mouth like she was exhaling under water.

The last couple of hours had aged Daddy's little girl about ten years. Her eyes had fuck-me-I'm-easy shadows under them and there were sharp little lines on either side of her mouth which for once wasn't twisted in a smirk. Just a poor little rich girl nobody wanted to fuck. She was wearing an ankle-length black cashmere coat open over the same tight-fitting skirt she'd had on at Fellini's. How had she found me? A safe bet was that she was drawn to the lights on at Bill's on her way home.

She kept moving closer, eyes on my chest, almost like she couldn't see me standing in front of her. About six inches from my chin she stopped. A pill of ash loosened at the end of my cigarette and fell down her face. Then she looked up into my eyes.

"Once a prick always a prick," she said. She slipped her hand through my shirt over my heart and slowly moved it down my stomach and inside my pants, raking me with her nails. Between Susan and Donna, Jack Shock's manhood was having quite a night of it.

She looked up at me slyly, that crooked smirk glinting in the lamplight.

Like Susan, Donna was not above hyperbole, to get her way with old Jack.

"I'd almost forgot how big you get," she said.

"It's hooked up to a bicycle pump."

I exhaled and shook another pill of ash down the cleft of her breasts. Once a prick and all that. Oh, she was still a hottie, scowl lines and all. But it wasn't that keeping me in Donna's grasp, so to speak, just the old one-two of loathing and self-loathing that had served me so well all these years. Right now loathing had the upper hand. I wished she was not just dead but dead and able to feel dental pain. But I stayed hard anyway, the old meat having its way with the old brain that should have known better.

I heard the frozen grass crunching behind me and turned. Like a doe caught in the headlights, Susan stumbled towards us with startled eyes. The hand jive didn't stop; this was the sort of moment Donna lived for. I got back. Donna took a deep drag and blew it into my face. Susan glared at us, pure cat.

"Susan," I said, "this is my better half, Donna, of whom you've surely heard me speak." "Donna, this is Susan Monteith." The absurd formality of my speech grated in my ears. "You know. The student you told Bernie I was fucking for a grade."

Donna looked Susan up and down. "What did she get? A C-plus?"

"An A-minus actually," Susan said.

"Oh," Donna said, "I didn't realize you were giving head too. Did you swallow or spit? If you swallowed, you definitely should have gotten the A."

As far as I knew, Susan hadn't heard the first thing about Vandillingham's crusade against womanizers like Jack Shock, but she was a quick study. For a long moment the two of them stood there looking each other over. Finally, Donna took a cigarette out of her coat pocket and lit it with the little gold lighter that Daddy Prileau had given her, the one with a big D worked in lapis lazuli. She took her time. I was hoping that Susan would lay one upside her head. But she turned to me instead.

"Are you with her?" Susan asked, giving me a straight look.

"Never again."

I ducked as Donna's cigarette once again came flying right at my eyes.

"*Good* shot," said a voice behind me. It was Drew, the Poetry Man. Donna's Virginia Slim glowed in his right hand. He took a drag.

"You'd best use a rubber," I said. "No telling what she's had in her mouth lately."

"You mother fucker," Donna said and threw the lighter at me. I caught it left-handed, leaned over and dropped it in her pocket.

"To be continued, Lambie-Pie," I stage-whispered in her ear.

She turned on her three-hundred-dollar heels and stepped into the darkness, getting a nice little sideways action from the stilettos, the anger, the booze, and whatever other chemical supplements she'd taken that night — cocaine, if I knew my girl. Oh well. A couple of blocks, home, and she'd lose her mad in white powder oblivion.

"Nighty-night, Donna dearest." I called after her.

"Susan," from his tone you could tell that Drew was taking the high road, "do you really want to go home tonight with *this*?" He was pointing at me like I was a dog turd on his beach towel. Good question. It just wasn't Drew's night. Susan had every reason to walk. She was mad alright, but not walking away mad. She wasn't going to cut me loose until she had spoken her piece.

"Drew," I said. "Why don't you go back in there and play with Bill. Or better yet, give Bernie a blow job and get a lock on the whole tenure thing."

Drew looked positively savage, started to say something, thought better of it and made another of his bloody-but-unbowed exits.

I looked at Susan and she looked at me. For a while neither of us said anything.

"What's this about my" — she was the kind of girl who never says *fuck* — "sleeping with you for a grade?"

So I told her. She listened, not liking it much.

"What about you and your wife — of whom I have surely heard you speak?" she asked, nodding towards the dark into which Donna had gone walking.

"That was over before you and I got started."

"It didn't look over five minutes ago," she said.

She had me there. When I didn't say anything, she went on.

"And what about the one you're in love with, the one in Washington?"

That was the sixty-four-thousand-dollar question, all right. None of the rest of it mattered much alongside that one. Not the job, not all the trouble Donna could make for me, not my cabin in the pines. Not even, God bless her, lovely Susan. I didn't say anything but I must have looked almost as bad as I felt, because Susan stood on her tiptoes and kissed me on both cheeks. "Poor Jack," she said. It felt like the sweetest thing she had ever done for me. "Come on," she said, linking her arm through mine. "I'll take you to your car."

12. *Mr. Highwayman*

Mr. Highwayman, please don't block my road.

Cause she registerin' a cold one hundred.

And I'm booked and I got to go.

Robert Johnson

After Susan dropped me off, I stood there in the parking lot leaning against the hood of the Continental. It was some hood. They had stamped it out in Detroit back in the days when sheet metal meant something. There was a motor under that hood the size of a deep freezer. It could sure suck down the gas, and it wanted nothing but the best, the hundred octane kind if they still made anymore.

It had gone cloudy again. The scimitar moon was sheathed in dark clouds, not a star in sight. A dust of snow came spinning down, whirled by the wind, looking fake as the movie set at the beginning of *Citizen Kane* — when young Kane finds out he's a millionaire and doesn't want to leave home and Rosebud.

I stood there a long while thinking about the botch I'd made of my first day back on the job. "Botch" didn't quite seem to do it justice. Here I was two years later about to throw myself into the breach again, twice as miserable as I was when I'd run away from the botch I'd made of my life before this new botch. I'd managed to alienate just about everyone I'd met who didn't already loathe me. Tomorrow I was supposed to start the course in Chessnuts of Dixie. With my luck the hyphenated chick would be sitting next to me. What a drag.

And then, saving the best for last, there was Sam. What the hell was I going to do about that one? What lies or truth could I tell to save us the hell I knew both of us were going to go through before RIP was spoken over the grave our love had become. Try to think of a new word for incest, Jack. A euphemism. The love that would just as soon not tell its name, now that the Oscar Wilde kind was positively chi-chi even in far-from-the-madding-crowd Charlottesville. Let's sit down to dinner with that one, Jack. Just you and Sam and the moonless winter night.

While I was thinking this or something like it, a white-white car wove across the parking lot crackling gravel, one of Charlottesville's finest behind the wheel, stalking the children of the night. I must have looked like a pretty good bet. Hell, I was. I felt as bloody-minded as Hamlet after he sends the two frat boys off to instant death in England.

The cop who got out from behind the wheel was fat and very young, maybe a couple of years out of high school. He leveled a flashlight at me big enough to cold-cock a rhino, some kind of halogen, beam-me-up-Scotty space-age torch. The light from it flat blinded me. Maybe he'd ordered it from one of those paramilitary catalogues, the ones with pages and pages of killer knives, all of them with names and pedigrees: Rambo One, The Bruce Lee Throwing Star, Terminator. And pages of squiggly bladed krisses, scimitars, gurkas, Scots daggers and a whole page of bowie knives, each of them at least the size of the Continental's tire tool.

His broad moon of a face shone white as a catfish belly in the gleam of the headlight and his nose was freckled and beaded with sweat. I was staring at his name tag. I couldn't tell whether it really said Robert Johnson, a mind-fucker from old McFate, or whether my eyes were just playing tricks on me.

"Put your hands where I can see them," he said, speaking in a kinked up accent from one of the southwest coal mining counties. His right hand rested on the butt of a big magnum revolved in a snap-down holster. Pretty damn quick I did what he said, hoping Robert didn't have a wild hair up his ass tonight. Because I sure as hell did.

"Is this your vehicle?" he asked, pronouncing it like it rhymed with pickle. I answered that it was.

"Let me see your license, sir." Uncharacteristically, I did have my license in my wallet and I fished it out for him. I caught a glimpse of my face reflected in the Lincoln's window. I was wearing one of those smiles that people come up with who don't know any better, who haven't figured out that life will break your heart. I held out a plastic version of the same smile and he took it from me like it was something dead. He looked it over for a good thirty seconds before he handed it back to me.

"You got a registration for this vehicle?" I said I thought there might be one in the glove box.

"Would you mind getting it out for me, sir?"

He was certainly covering his ass with sirs. Maybe he went to the same academy of manners as the orange-haired bus driver on the zoo line. When I reached into the glove box the first thing I put my hand on was a .45 automatic, the old man's sidearm from W.W. Two. For an instant my hands closed round the pistol grip. An impulse flashed through me, straight out of Poe to pull it out and to reenact the last seven minutes of *The Wild Bunch*. I imagined the white moon of Officer Robert Johnson's face describing a slow motion arc as he crumpled to the blacktop, in one of those vintage Peckinpah, snail-paced, ultra violent shots. Underneath the pistol was my ticket to sanity, the registration for the Continental. My fingers chose that instead. That wild hair just wasn't quite wild enough.

Again Officer Johnson took the card from my hand like it was a piece of three-day-old catfish bait. And he looked it over like it was a lottery ticket he was going to have to pay out of his own pocket. Then he handed it back to me with a great show of decorum.

"You, a general?" he said looking at the big star on the Continental's bumper. He was looking at my almost black, disrespectable bearded face with wide open incredulity.

"My old man," I explained.

He nodded. "Didn't think you was." He sighed theatrically. "Sir, these parking lots are specifically off-limits for any kind of social activity after the hour of ten o'clock."

I nodded, wondering just what social activity he thought I was engaged in.

"Have you had anything to drink tonight, sir, I mean of an alcoholic nature?"

I nodded yes.

"How much?"

"Don't remember," I said, not trying to.

"How long ago?"

"What time is it now?"

He pulled back his sleeve to look at one of those oversized, multifunction, black plastic quartz diver's watches that people buy who wouldn't even take a bath wearing them.

"Two o'clock."

"Four hours ago, I guess."

"Would you mind taking a breathalyzer test, sir."

"Sure," I said. "I wouldn't mind knowing what legally drunk feels like, for future reference, I mean, as opposed to just plain drunk."

Officer Johnson gave me one of those "you smart ass" looks I can inspire in authority figures almost without trying. He got the thingamabob out of the car. I breathed into it and he took it back to his car with a display of ceremony all out of proportion to the occasion. He talked indistinctly into his car phone awhile and came back wearing a disgusted look.

"Sir, you are as close to legally drunk as you can be and still drive."

"My lucky day," I said.

"You're free to go," he said. "But I advise you to get into your vehicle and drive slowly" — he said the word like the lady on Romper Room — "to wherever you got to get to tonight."

I nodded. He got into his car and waited rather ostentatiously for me to fire up the Continental and roll. The big motor started on the first try, just like the old man's cars always did, and I drove it towards that cloud bank to the east where the moon was still hiding.

13. Love in Vain

When the train pulled out the station
had two lights on behind.
The blue light was my baby
and the red light was my mind.

Robert Johnson

The road ran deep and moonless as an asphalt river through the mountains. The Continental felt like a big white raft gliding down it ultra slow, a long forever before and behind. Here and there the sky was peppered with bird shot points of light. I couldn't believe I'd actually thought about shooting a cop just to break into a different way of miserable. I was in a hell of a place. Step on a crack. Kill what you love. Blues falling down like hail.

Maybe the old man was up there among the stars looking down now with maybe Mom and Sam and Annie, not watching over me, just watching, as if they could see me and my destination whatever it might be at the same time, knowing how it would end with Sam, with Donna, with Susan. All of it. Watching and not especially anxious. Why would he be? He was out of what I was in. They all were. And to them it would all seem pretty damn pointless.

It wasn't pointless to me though. I could remember how angry I'd been after I read the letter, though I knew even then that the old man couldn't have foreseen what had come to pass. Donna had seen it coming a long way off. But not the old man. Vivid imagination wasn't one of his afflictions. I thought of how lonely his life must have been after mom had died. Whatever he'd found in Aunt Grace's arms, I hoped there had been love too. At the end he was trying to make it right with me, father to son. If I was fucked, it wasn't his doing, anymore than it was Sam's. Just the purblind doomsters again, half-drunk, missing the dart board, not to mention the bull's-eye.

All of a sudden I needed a drink. I was pretty sure there was a fifth of Jim Beam in my B-4 bag. I hit the brakes a shade too hard, gravel flying and slid to a stop at the foot of Diggs Mountain. The way my mind was working I wasn't sure I'd find the bottle, but, McFate be thanked, it was there. The liquor filled my throat with fire and ice. I leaned back against the trunk and drank again looking up into the bird shot blanket of the night. Here's to you, I said, to no one. Here's to you too, I said drinking again, thinking of the old man. Like old Mr. Flood in the poem saying good night to his graveyard of personal ghosts. Then I heard crunching gravel behind me. Frozen in the headlights was a doe. She had stumbled down the hillside and she stood there steaming, with trout pool eyes. I thought of Susan. I thought of Sam. What I had to tell her, like all great blistering truths, was something that would stop her in her tracks. "Sam," I said aloud. The doe never moved. I leaned in the door and cut off the headlights. For a moment she stood there, a shadow in the darkness. Then I heard the scuff of hooves on the macadam, the whisper of winter-dry brush. When I turned the lights on again she was gone.

I sat on the Continental hood drinking the whiskey. I tried moon dreaming an easy way out of it with Sam, maybe stonewalling it, shoving her back into Charley Boy's arms. I would call her up and say it had all been a big mistake. Just one of those things. It just wouldn't have worked. There's this other woman. Whatever cheeseballs say to their own true loves when they shoot them in the head at moments like these. And she'd believe it. No doubt of that. Because deep down who believes the real thing will ever come his way? We settle for convenience, contentment, a good lay (witness my own case), some half life of love, convincing ourselves it's what we really wanted anyway. She'd believe it was just more of life's bullshit. That's what she got for loving me; I'd cut her sweet heart out, douse it with gas and set it on fire. Anything but tell her the truth.

But when I tried to fashion the knife-edged words, they just wouldn't come. I knew I'd never pull it off. She'd come down from D.C. and somehow she'd get it out of me. Not by wheedling. But she'd see I still loved her. She'd see it, all right. And she wouldn't give up without a fight. That's what I told myself anyway.

I took another drink. What were my options? An arm's length away in the glove box, three pounds of steel, a slight contraction of the index finger. A paint bucket of brains and blood on the mountainside, frozen by morning. That was option one.

Well forget that one. I was no antique Roman. I was a great believer in the metaphysics of beer commercials and a student of Ovid and Herrick to boot. I wasn't ready to pitch in my hand for good. As long as there was reefer and whiskey and the fair sex left in the world, I'd hang in for the next hand. As a life admittedly it was a shallow rill, but I didn't have the nuts to fall on my sword, a few lines of blank verse tripping from my lips.

Option two. Make a run for the border. These days lighting out for the territories meant coconuts and killer bees, fer de lances and fire ants. Give me a home where the tarantulas roam among the stately banana trees. Maybe I start my own fucking country. King Jack. President Shock. I took a drink. What the old man had left me would do for a couple of lifetimes in Belize or Costa Rica — at least the way I lived. It would last four or five times that long in Guatemala. Maybe I wouldn't go alone. Maybe I'd ask Susan to make the trip with me. On second thought if she wanted me that bad, there had to be some sick in it somewhere. I was sick enough myself for five or six sane women without needing more of it, thanks. So, aloha, and God bless, sweet Susan.

Sam's face flashed into my mind, deer soft eyes smiling. I just went all to pieces. The tears rolled down in big drops and when I looked down after a while my shirt was wet as a dishrag. I hadn't cried like that a handful of times since I was a little kid. The first time I found out Donna was cheating on me. When they played "Taps" over the old man's grave. They say it does you good. Don't you believe it. It's just anesthesia, what the gazelle feels in the lion's grasp. Some good. I took a belt of my preferred brand of painkiller. Then I got in, shoved the bottle under the seat and slipped the Continental in gear. The tape came on. "I got a kind-hearted woman, anything is worse for me." I hit the fast forward. "Keep moving. Blues falling down like hail." Bob again, better than your horoscope. I turned it off and drove the rest of the way home in silence.

I had the feeling turning down the sunken, rutted, clay-colored lane that led to the cabin that I was driving into one of those dreams I'd had in Washington, the one that had pushed me into Sam's arms. There at the first curve was the crooked, scale-barked wild cherry, the one I had bent the road around to save. Something struck me funny about that road. It seemed smoother than it should have been. Where there should have been gullies after two years of rain-fed erosion, there were shallow side ditches. And the road was crowned and banked. And when I reached the two metal posts I'd set in concrete to hang a chain between, the chain lay flat, not like it had been cut but like it had been unlocked. Then I remembered who would have the key.

I can't say I knew what I'd find when I got to the cabin, but I knew when I saw Sam's car, one of those sawed-off Toyotas with a door in the back, that it seemed like the whole day had been tending towards this moment. Vandillingham in all his epicene mediocrity. The Letter From The Grave. Round one with Donna. Susan and the Thumbheads. Bill Smalls, going down slow. But seeing Sam's car was worse than all the rest of it put together. I got out and leaned on the Continental's roof. The lights of the cabin streamed into the blackness like searchers after truth, or what passed for it among such as Jack Shock. A plume of white smoke, of cured red oak by the smell of it, scented the night, for all the sick terror of this moment, with something like welcome. I saw a shadow move behind the curtained window. The door opened. Sam stood framed in the jambs, her long hair streaming down, all alive with sparkles of light.

We watched each other across thirty yards of blackest night. All my life I'd been a specialist at shoving it under the bed; drinking or smoking it to sleep; moving on to the next bit. I'd told myself I'd gotten to the point where I didn't feel the sting anymore. Well, I'd known the moment I clapped eyes on her in Washington that I'd just been kidding myself. Right now, it felt like some Norse Shield Warrior had taken his battle axe and cleaned my legs out from under me. I sat back down in the car just looking at my hands. Then I saw that they were wet and I could tell that my face had gotten wet too. I was doing it again. I wasn't blubbering, but I wouldn't stop the water. It was the saddest crying I've ever done.

I looked up and saw Sam standing beside me. She knelt down and I could see that she was shivering a little from the cold. All she had on was one of my old sweaters and a pair of jeans. She didn't say anything. She put her arms around my neck and touched her forehead to my temple, lightly, almost like a kiss. I could feel her tears on my neck. She shook and shivered but she never whimpered. The cold wind slicing through my open coat made me think of that letter stabbing at my heart. I knew I should speak, but I just couldn't find the words. I couldn't even find the strength to say her name.

"Is it us?" She asked after a long time.

Well that was an opening if I'd ever heard one, even for a man with a heart of wood.

"What's wrong, Jack?"

What ain't, I thought, except you, my love. Because she was all right, Sam was. She was a world beater. I could drain wells of purple ink and all the poetry there is and it wouldn't touch what she was to me at that moment. God knows I didn't give a fuck about anything else. I didn't know whether what I owed her was the truth or protection from it. So I didn't say anything. After a while though I could feel her shivering and shaking against me so that I thought that she would break apart. Poor baby, I thought. I didn't dare say it.

I made her get up then and walked her to the house. The door was still open. Fire danced in the glass window of the Old Defiant. Just seeing fire can make you feel warmer, but it didn't me. Not that night.

I looked around. It was a way to keep from looking at her. The hewn oak logs bedded in chinking mud the color of river sand. The heart pine floor of random width boards, some of them as wide as book shelves, and studded with old rosehead nails, glowed as red as the fire. On the north wall was a poster-sized photograph of Robert Johnson. The one in which he's got the beat-to-hell, round-butted 1928 Gibson L-I on his lap. He's wearing a smile and a gray fedora slanted raffishly and a flashy suit like the one Joe Christmas has on when he first shows up at the planing mill. Sam had probably gotten the poster made in D.C.

She followed my eyes but she didn't speak. She waited well, better than I could have. And God she had never looked so beautiful. Maybe I thought that because I was just about to break her heart. Or maybe, like another drunk said once, it was pretty to think so.

I was starting to feel the absurdity of my silence. Why didn't I just come out with it? Why didn't I tell her about the old man's letter? I knew I could make her believe that I believed that it was true. Still I said nothing.

She was looking at me as if her heart had already broken. Her face wet, her eyes glittering, her lips parted.

"Tell me, Jack," she said.

"It's over," I heard my voice say.

"Over," she said brokenly.

"Like yesterday," the voice said.

"You don't love me anymore?" she was pleading. You'd need a heart of stone to turn your back on that voice, that face.

"No," I said.

"You said you wanted to marry me."

I couldn't look at her. I stared into the fire.

"No postmortems," the voice said. It was a faraway voice that never broke.

She walked to the door, walked out of it, leaving it open. She didn't say goodbye.

I heard her car start up; it sounded like it needed a muffler. Then she was gone. It was a long time before I got up to shut the door. The fire had burned to embers. It was that that roused me, though not from sleep. The sun was rising. It was the light that I had to shut out. I didn't want to look into any corners. I'd had my share of looking into corners for one night. The dark and cold surrounded me again as I sat shivering in the old cane-bottomed chair, rocking and rocking before the dying fire.

14. I Looked Out the Mountain

I looked out the mountain, far as I could see
Some man had my woman
And the lonesome blues had me.

Robert Johnson

About a month after Sam drove off into the dark and left me to the misery I called my life, some thoughtful soul — Donna no question about it — her hand was dayglo in the very idea of it — sent me the wedding announcements page from the *Post*. The image burned into my brain like a brick red iron: Charley-Boy, smug, his arm around her waist.

Sam smiling, I tried to keep from looking at the date, the place, but I couldn't bring myself to crumple up her paper face the way I had her real one. I couldn't bring myself to throw the paper away either and in the end I looked. April twenty-third it said, St. Swithins. It was, I decided, probably a high church Episcopalian, elegy-written-in-a-country-churchyard congregation that sang God Save the Queen at the end of every service. A place where Charley-Boy was accepted as heir apparent to the Windsor throne, switched at birth with his jug-eared namesake.

Every time I thought about her was an acid bath washing down my heart. The cure I was taking had failed to achieve the desired effect. The bourbon cure, I mean, Dr. J. Beam presiding. Like a train whistle, the memory of her face, her smile would gleam through the fog of whatever hangover I was trying to drink myself out of. I can't say that I drank because of any illusion that I would escape the ganglia of pain in my skull. But once I started to belt down whatever bottled cure I was taking that night, I never quit until I dropped like a felled beef.

That's how it was ever after. I sentenced myself to a blackout drunk in solitary confinement in my cabin, one morning, if that's what time it really was. I was jarred awake by the ringing of the telephone and I ripped it out of the wall. It stayed in a heap in the corner of the cabin all winter. The mail carrier, noticing I'd come home, placed a box the size of a small refrigerator filled with two years of dead letters blocking the entrance to my road. I dumped it into the back of the Continental. My new mail stayed in the mailbox until pieces of it started spilling into the side ditch. I gathered them up and threw them into the cascade in the back seat. Then at the urging of the departmental secretary, I took my office mail out to the car and dumped it so that letters spilled down into the floor boards like the detritus from a spent volcano.

Sometime in early March the power company sent a uniformed emissary by the nametag of Bud to switch off the electricity. He was very apologetic about it. All I had to do was pay my bill. Well, thanks, Bud, and so forth I remember myself saying. I never got around to it. Amazing how little effect the lack of electricity had on my life. When nature called I staggered out the backyard and into the woods until I blundered into a tree while I shook the dew off my lily. Eating I more or less gave up on altogether. Now and again, usually when I filled up the Continental's twenty-five-gallon tank, I'd grab a bag of something that crunched when it went down. The crunch made it feel more like food. I don't remember much about brands and so forth. None of it made any impression on my taste buds. I'd get this raw feeling in my gut, from the whiskey, and something dry and bulky and weightless seemed to help, like sawdust on a pool of oil on a concrete floor.

Besides the cure, I didn't drink much. When I needed it, I fetched water from the spring. Very damn little of it at that. The house was as dark as a cave. Even after the wood gave out, I spent most of my time sleeping by the stove in an old Morris chair, drinking whatever I'd taken a notion to shove into the cart at the ABC store. Something dark, like Jim Beam. I chain-dragged Camel shorts and when I ran out I'd fish the butts out of ashtrays and corners and smoke them on toothpicks like roaches.

The only social intercourse I permitted myself was teaching. But really that was part of the sentence too. The first day of classes I had the shakes so bad when I opened the door of the car that I had to drink half of a fifth of Bushmills just to keep my eyes screwed in tight. Walking across the parking lot, I felt every step in my teeth; the pebbly surface felt like stalagmites piercing the soles of my shoes. The first person I saw when I walked through the door of McGregor Hall 222 was the hyphenated chick from Bill Small's Gotterdammerung party, pinning me to the wall with formaldehyde-colored eyes. As my eyes made a circuit around the room I noticed various odd-duck refugees from life. Welcome back to academia, Jack.

I discovered a chair behind the desk at the front of the class and sitting down in it spilled a tepid cup of bourbon-colored department coffee down my pants leg. It looked like my left testicle was having a long brown cry. Funnily enough I erupted into a stream of thank-God-no-one-can-hear-me curses which of course everyone could. It hit me suddenly that this was the Old South course. Mississippi looked like the place to start. I launched into a description of the Delta in the thirties. Stovall's Plantation. Thousands of blacks in a feudal ex-jungle working the land for a white overlord they never saw, living in shanties that would have been condemned and burnt in tribal Africa, making twenty-five cents an hour if they were lucky. That was the theme of my diatribe. I heard myself saying that West Mississippi must have been as impenetrable as West Africa when Kurtz went up the Congo in the 1890s. I continued in that vein, a jungle of ideas impenetrable even to myself — the Bushmills kicking in strong. I found myself talking about Robert

Johnson. Surprise, surprise. Of how his voice and music represented the linguistic counterpart to the Delta. (I think I said "linguistic" just to kowtow; the fish-eyed stares were starting to get to me the more I got out there.) The Africans of Ita Bena or Clarksdale or Stovalls Plantation cultivating an opacity of speech intended to confound the heirs of the race that had enslaved them. I think I jungled on in that vein in a semi-brownout with an increasing opacity of my own, identifying with the black Deltans and succeeding no doubt in boring my post-modern overseers if not in confounding them.

I found myself bird dogging my favorite prey in earnest, the non plus ultras of opacity, those lunatic Genevaites, those generalissimos of gender, the whole froggy crew and their patented p.c. ethos. It was not, I decided later, a fortunate choice. After the first batch of papers I figured it out. I had blundered into a grouping of students like one of those chocolate chip cookies that are all chips. And in this case the chips were all Vandillinghamites, post-modern to the core. Had my old buddy Bernie bribed or coerced this band of Venutians into taking my class? Once the paranoiac fog had dissipated, I decided that Venutians were standard issue for that year. Maybe in a fleeting moment of lucidity I recognized that along with more liquor than was good for me, or a platoon of me for that matter, I had enough of the death wish syndrome sloshing around in my head to fuck up a class of sighted and hearing Helen Kellers. Worthless to them, I was even more worthless to myself. It wasn't even a case of going through the motions. I was too far gone even to remember the motions.

The undergraduates I didn't mind so much. They weren't any trouble. My first day in MacGregor 431 I stood at a podium beside a desk and chair facing a room filled with baseball-capped heads sloping towards me as I talked about whatever floated by at ten o'clock in the morning on a Tuesday or a Thursday. One long solipsistic dialogue. The semester before I returned, someone had had the foresight or taken the liberty of ordering texts for the course, assuming not without some warrant that I wasn't going to be around to teach it. There was even a syllabus, printed up with her name on it. All that semester students left me notes addressed to Professor Michele Pincus. A couple of times a student called me Mr. Pincus. It was another one of those contretemps I never got around to shedding light on. Michele, by the way, or Mike as she preferred to be called, looked and dressed like a biker, with the tattoos to go with the look, had gone to Smith, had gotten her doctorate at CCNY, and had a whole different angle on vision of the twentieth century than the one inhabited by the Dead White Males I taught. Mike's reading list was top heavy with the *Wide Sargasso Sea* crew. I ignored the books I didn't remember and lectured on others that I never got around to ordering for the class.

That was the complaint that floated back to me in a memo from Vandillingham. *Dark Laughter* was out of print and had been for years. And who the hell taught Sherwood Anderson anymore? I was also teaching Dreiser

— whom Vandillingham called Theodore the Unreadable — *An American Tragedy* to be precise, replaying it in my mind's eye with Jack as Clyde and Sam as Roberta, although giving Jack Shock his due, he had loved his Roberta. I wrote Bernie back that when I wanted an opinion on American literature I would give it to him and forget it. That was the last I heard from Bernie about my reading list.

Yes, on the whole, I liked my undergraduates. I especially liked the fact that most of them dropped the class. Never once did one of the myrmidons in baseball caps raise a hand to question the logic, not to say the sanity of the proceedings. There they sat, drinking me in like calves on the teat. Flattering. Except for the hats you'd have thought that they were moonlighting as woodcutters — L. L. Bean flannels and high-topped leather boots. Northern Exposure regalia, Bill Smalls called it one day when I ran into him in the windowless hall that conducted us to our assignations with the lumberjacks. Of the seventy odd faculty in the department he was the only one I blundered into with any regularity. He no longer held my promotion against me. And I now felt grateful to him for throwing himself on the grenade of Donna's sexual appetite.

Meanwhile the handful of souls who remained in Michele Pincus's aborted class sat patiently waiting to transcribe whatever, hanging on my every word, pens racing across the page. Every once in a while the absurdity of the scene would overtake me in mid-sentence and I'd break into my bad imitation of a laugh until the Camel cough I'd developed and couldn't shake would send me hacking and gagging to the window, where with a seismic hawk I would clear my throat and spit, unless necessity forced me to adopt the gruesome expediency of the trash can. After the fit had passed I'd look up at their baffled, mildly revolted, and yet always respectful faces. Did they mistake my unsanitary performance for the idiosyncrasy of genius? I doubted that mightily. Probably their reaction derived from timidity or indifference. As to what I said, well, God knows I don't remember any particulars. I stumbled through my paces in some kind of parody of the imitation of a professor I already was, deluding myself that I was just fine, glad for the diversion from my sentence.

True, the morning cakewalk with the baseball caps was always followed by the Deep South course at 2:30, a barefoot stagger down a glass-strewn escalator to hell. But in the end even the Venutians seemed as ordinary to me as a shot of Jim Beam in my coffee at six a.m. And so in this strange half light of understanding, Jack Shock awaited April, the cruelest month, in which Penelope betrothed to Charlie Bledsoe would pass from his life forever.

15. Going Down Slow

I've had my fun, if I don't get well no more.
My friends don't come round me
Cause I'm going down slow.

St. Louis Odum

After a month of wallowing in my freezing, dark, waterless cabin, I drove to the co-op and paid my electric bill. The no longer invisible bottles, crumpled packs of Camels, and the butts themselves had to be gotten up and dumped. I did all that. I didn't pay the phone bill. There was still no one I wanted to talk to. I continued to ignore the mail. The pile in the back seat of the Continental filled the floor space, spilling onto the front armrest.

One day I fired up the General's ancient McCullough, the size of a Harley Davidson Flat Head without the wheels. I bucked and split and racked a granddaddy oak that had tumbled across the driveway a hundred feet or so from the cabin. It was the first real work I'd done in two years. So now there was something else in the house besides cigarettes to burn.

Every day except Sunday I drove to the ABC Store and bought another fifth of something brown, Jim Beam if they had it. Then I stopped at Shady's Place and bought a couple packs of Camel shorts. I kept a can of Bugler and some Tops cigarette papers for emergencies. There was still never anything to eat in the cabin. I ate what little I ate in gas stations and bars.

I preferred to drink at Fellini's and Whitey's. When snow kept me home, I sat in the old Morris chair staring into the fire, trying to prove to myself algebraically that I had done right by Sam. I tried never to let her face light up my mind. For I was no good to her. She was better off with Charley-Boy. That phrase was always as far as I thought, bitter though it was to end there.

I never actually reread the old man's letter, but more or less, I had it memorized. One phrase haunted me. He had trusted in my probity. Of all the words in the dictionary, that one had the least to do with the mess I'd made of things.

My brand of probity had inflicted on her a pain at least as great as my own, without granting her the knowledge that made the bearing of it possible for me. I did not believe I would see her face again. In that one thing, I had succeeded. In a month — or so the announcement had read — she and Charley-Boy would marry. I tried to convince myself that if I could drink myself up to and past that day, a milestone would have been passed. Right. Just an excuse to drink, as if I needed one.

It might have gone on like that until my liver gave out. But McFate had reserved for me a day that I had pretended would never come if I just didn't read my mail. It was the first Tuesday in March. My 2:30 class in Chessnuts of Dixie had limped to a forgone conclusion. Eudora Welty was done for. Six down. Four to go. I'd only assigned the one paper. I was so depressed after reading them I decided to spare myself another batch. As I escaped to the hallway puffing on a cigarette, the hyphenated woman assailed me, begging me to assign a second essay, to schedule an examination.

Precisely in the middle of the hallway stood McFate in the person of Bernard Vandillingham blocking my path to the Continental where Jim Beam awaited hiding under the seat.

"Professor Shock," he said.

I took note of his tone, deep and oracular, quite unlike his normally shrill speaking voice. It struck me that I couldn't remember the last time someone had addressed me by my professional title.

"The same," I said, not a hint of quaver in that voice.

"You have an appointment to keep," he said.

I said nothing. I didn't know whether I knew what the hell he was talking about. These days, I forgot a lot. The students who had followed me out and a couple of passers-by had pooled around us. They looked from Bernie to me as if a "Doctor Livingston, I presume" moment was imminent. I waited.

"We are waiting for you in the Bowers Library," he said.

This was news to me. A sentence from *Tom Jones* popped into my head: "Hide, and if they find you, lie."

"Sorry," I said, tapping my lower jaw. "I'm on my way to the dentist. Pretty sure I've got a root canal coming on."

Pleased with myself and wincing for effect, I actually pushed past old Bernie towards the hollow, battleship gray double door, vintage Sing-Sing by the look of it. As he stepped involuntarily back, I looked Bernie in the eye with all the insincerity I could muster while smiling a crooked little smile that would have done Donna dearest proud.

"Shock," he barked, "You have been summoned to a departmental inquiry . . ."

"*Professor* Shock to you," I muttered pseudoindignantly. I was through the doors. Bernie's barking sounded like gurgling. I bolted across Jefferson Park Avenue, despite the protests of horns and brakes. Then I was in the sanctuary of the parking lot.

Sitting in the Continental, pint of Jim Beam in hand, I recollected that, yes, there had been a sign on the Bowers Library door this morning. Quite a large one. Phrases like "Reserved for Official University Business" and "Do not attempt to enter after five o'clock" lent authority to Bernie's impersonation of McFate. Come to think of it, Old Bernie was looking more pompous than usual, all in black, like Susan's Drew, as if he were going to a funeral. Mine, it seemed.

Touching the bottle's mouth to my own, I took a long glug. The tension in my neck gave way, and the prickles in my scalp grew calm. I glanced over my shoulder at a cardboard box brimming with envelopes embedded in the avalanche of envelopes on the rear seat. One of the academic secretaries had placed that box in my hands with a knowing smile as I was on my way out a week or so ago. I had nestled it in the back seat and hadn't given it a thought since. I had the feeling that her smirk, the vaguely ominous sign on the Bowers Library door, and Bernie's presence outside my door a few minutes ago were linked and could all be explained by one of those envelopes, probably the one with the faintly greenish tint that usually contained important institutional announcements.

"Fucking A" I said aloud between glugs of Jim Beam. "No. Fucking Bernie." A couple more glugs later I was reading the thing itself.

Dear Professor Shock:

This letter is to inform you that you are required to appear before a Departmental Court of Enquiry into your conduct during the last two semesters in which you taught at this University. There are two charges.

1) First, that you engaged in sexual relations with an undergraduate student during the spring semester before you went on sabbatical.

2) Second, that your conduct in the present semester in both your undergraduate and graduate classes has been unprofessional in the extreme and worthy of censure. The time and date of this enquiry have been set for 5:00 p.m. on Tuesday, March 5, in the Bowers Library. You should collect all materials pertaining to these charges and bring them with you to the enquiry described above.

Very truly yours,

Bernard Vandillingham

Chair, Department of English

The University of Virginia

Well, there it was. "Here's to you, Bernie," I said, nodding at the green envelope on the dashboard and finishing the pint in one swallow, "Vandillingham may be a good dog, but Jack Shock is a better one."

I knew for a fact, for instance, that Bernie couldn't fire me just because he hated my guts, good dog though he was. He could bark and snarl but he couldn't actually sink his teeth into my hide, poor old bowser. All he could do was gum me.

Take the first charge. Had I in fact indulged in sexual congress with one of my students? Yes, I had, if he meant Susan Monteith. Often in fact. But was she my student when said acts occurred? Or more importantly, was she then an undergraduate? There was the rub, Bernie. At the critical moment she was not a student at all, having finished her coursework the week before. It was not caution that had saved me this or any other time. Just blind luck. After lovely Susan had gone on to enroll in graduate school at the University, our liaison had gone into overdrive, Donna having moved out to move in with good old Bill. Alas for Bernie. The University in its infinite wisdom in matters touching the relations of professor and student did not proscribe the flagrantly sexual relationship I then enjoyed with Susan Monteith. The difference between "graduate" and "undergraduate" was Bernie's Waterloo.

I would have to prove all this of course. But I knew I could. And I knew that Bernie could not prove the contrary. So unless Susan had gone over to the dark side and was willing to lie to ruin me or to benefit herself, a thing not to be imagined, I was home free on charge one.

As to the second item, yes, I was guilty as charged. For a long time now my performance in the classroom had been a parody of teaching. But come now, Bernie. How many others among my colleagues were as guilty as Jack Shock of similar travesties? Day after day, year after year, class after class until the last syllable of recorded time, professors had badgered, insulted, belittled and most of all bored their students to dusty death. It was a cliché, for Christ's sake. Not necessarily because like Jack Shock they were stinko or blotto or sloshed but because they were tedious fools with the egos of Napoleon and no more talent for fascinating an audience than the average high school valedictorian. Not every damn one of them, of course, but plenty enough. And most of this plenty were only as fascinating as the phone book on a good day and as a car rental agreement on a bad one. So Bernie could crack corn. Jack Shock didn't care. Charge two had gone away.

This was cause for celebration. Fellini's beckoned. The one bar in town that kept a barstool reserved just for me.

16. Blues Walking Like a Man

And the blues fell, mama's child

And they tore me all upside down.

Robert Johnson

The day had cooled and the sky had turned a purple brown as I stood at the glass doored entrance to Fellini's watching my breath steaming it up. It said a lot that for the last two months I'd spent more time in Fellini's than in the house I'd built with my own hands.

I had my reasons. Fellini's was a place where they wrote your name on the Jim Beam bottle in the ice chest. Where the lighting was more like candles than strobes. Where everybody smoked. Where no matter how much you drank, they never cut you off. Where you could reinvent yourself for the night. Where they never asked you why you felt the need to get blotto night after night.

They caught on early that I had a favorite barstool, the one seat in the house where you couldn't see your face in the long mirror that framed the wall behind the bartender. When I caught sight of my black-bearded face, it was like a face glimpsed in a crowd that I couldn't put a name to. It made me think of the self-portrait of Rembrandt in the National Gallery. How fleeting was reputation, how constant vicissitude. A post-modernist alternative reading was that his face was no more Rembrandt than Hamlet was Shakespeare, or than Jack's smiling face was Jack Shock, outcast from life's feast.

Two weeks ago I'd come in to find sitting on my seat someone whom I'd taught in the old days when I still gave a damn. He was a lawyer now, enthusiastically drunk and happy with himself.

"Mr. Shock," he said, "God, I would never have thought I'd have run into you in a place like this."

His eyes took inventory. Chief, the owner and founder in his white tuxedo, forensically cheerful as always. Miss Fluffy, bored, in something skin tight. Plunkett digging into the ice chest with a cigarette in his mouth and five shots of Jim Beam in a silvery cocktail shaker that he was about to pour into a highball glass destined for none other than me.

"Why don't you leave then, Mr. Ryan," I said, "if this place doesn't suit you."

He took hold of my lapel, and I brushed his hands aside. I didn't have time for his summing up of my life. As if he had earned the right.

"Don't touch me, Mr. Ryan."

"You heard him, pal," Plunkett shouted, his hand resting on the brass fireplace poker he kept behind the bar. "If this place isn't good enough for you, run, don't walk, the fuck out of here."

Ryan staggered back, sending me a baffled look. The professor he'd once pretended to respect, was a barfly. Go figure. I felt like the fool I had been back then was looking at the drunken fool I'd become. Oh, well, I'd never much cared for heights, especially pedestals.

Some of this was fogging up my brain tonight as I decided to make my entrance. Plunkett turned towards me bellowing.

"Jack," he shouted. "I was just about to tell these two characters to move out of your seat."

Short, twenty-four, as round shouldered as a fireplug, wearing the smile of a cunning innocent, Plunkett muttered "Right . . . Right," while you talked if he liked you. If he didn't, he cocked his head back and stared at you balefully. He was definitely staring balefully at the two men at the bar.

"If it's his seat," said a tall, lank-haired country boy with a lot of sideways jaw movement, "Why ain't his name on it?" He stood up pointing at Plunkett with his cigarette hand, while he shoved the thumb of his other hand at me. A musty odor of sweat, cigarettes, and stale beer accompanied his movements. I sized him up as Jimber Jaws, the one who started the fights that the other one, shorter, darker, and sullen, finished.

Jimber Jaws wore a long frowzy topcoat of dark wool over a flannel shirt tucked into holey jeans with ragged cuffs over cracked Red Wing wellingtons. His hair and his teeth were long, yellow, and snaggled. Both needed brushing. A grubby Band-Aid held his left ear plastered to his skull and a filtered menthol cigarette outlined his gestures in smoke.

"Look, pal," Plunkett shouted, "you don't walk into a bar, order a beer, drink it, and bitch about the price. Pay up and get out."

This was Plunkett at the top of his game, never better than when outnumbered on the firing line.

The sullen one stood up. He wore a scuffed leather bomber jacket with a hole in the right elbow. A couple inches shorter than Jimber Jaws, he still had at least four inches on Plunkett.

"What are *you* going to do about it, piss pot," he said, in a hillbilly burr. His big knuckled hands gripped the bar as he leaned forward.

"What are *you* going to do about it, you sawed-off piss pot?" repeated Jimber Jaws, jabbing at Plunkett with his smoking hand.

Like Jove's thunderbolt, the poker came down on the glass ashtray between the two pals. Glass shards flew like shooting stars.

"*You* are going to fuck with *me*?" Plunkett shouted. His voice was like a wedding bell, shrill and joyful. He came around the bar with the poker cocked back in his hand like a harpoon. I had never seen him happier.

Ajax and Achilles pushed past me, the dark one dropping a ten on the floor as they ran out. Plunkett ignored the bribe and went after them, poker held high, running up Market Street, shouting "*You* are going to fuck with *me*?" at the top of his lungs. I stood at the door dragging down on a Camel watching until he chased them out of sight.

"There's Plunkett for you," said a Cockney voice behind me. It belonged to Victor, Fellini's cook. He was taking Plunkett's place behind the bar, his long gray-brown braid swinging.

"Ain't Plunkie served you a drink then, Jack?" he asked, reaching for the half-full bottle of Jim Beam in the ice chest. "Well, we'll fix that."

"Take one yourself," I said.

"No, Jack, not me. You like to drink, I like to smoke. Never the twain should mix."

He poured a stiff belt in a highball glass and I threw it down. I could feel the muscles of my neck beginning to relax.

"Another?" asked Victor, raising his eyebrows in a rhetorical question, already pouring.

"You know why I don't drink, Jack? The 'ard stuff, I mean — I do like me beer." I nodded. I had heard it all before. "I'll tell you." He took time to light the cigarette he'd extracted from the pack I extended towards him.

"Thanks, Jack." He looked at the cigarette. "I like the unfiltered ones. Taste better. Turkish?"

I nodded as he leaned back rocking on his heels.

"You got two chaps both in love with the same gel. They're talking about 'er and they're *drinking*. Pretty soon they're beating the shit out of each other."

He took a long drag on his cigarette.

"You take the same two chaps. Both in love with the same gel. They start talking about 'er. But this time they're *smoking*. Reefer! Ganja!Marijuana! And while they're talking about 'er, they both fall asleep."

He took another drag.

"And that's why I prefer the smoking to the drinking."

"Maybe Plunkie should try the smoking," I said.

"Good idea, Jack. Good idea."

The door swung open and Mick Reardon walked in.

"Fucking A, Jack. I just saw fucking Plunkett running up the street with the Fellini's poker in his hand chasing a couple of long-haired country boys."

"Did 'ee catch 'em?" asked Vic.

"He was gaining on them," said Mick. "Hey, Jack. Settling in for the night? Or do you want to go on tour?"

"On tour," I said.

Mick's choice for the first port-of-call was always what he called "That sleazy little fag bar." The Standard had the best looking waitresses, dressed hot and all in black. Since the clientele was mostly gay men, the odds, as Mick put it, were in our favor. I took his point. I was along just for the booze.

Usually, Mark Roebuck held court behind the bar but tonight, his old band mate, Skipper Brown, on sabbatical from Whitey's and dressed in what looked like a UVA black pajama uniform, stood before us with his blandly welcoming smile.

"The usual?" he asked me, already pouring it. After he was done, he set a spritzer with a twist of lemon before Mick.

"How long has it been?" Skipper asked Mick, nodding at the glass.

"Five years, last April 19," said Mick. "How long for you?"

"Eight," answered Skipper. He looked at me. "But Jack is drinking enough for both of us." "And then some," said Mick. We all laughed. Sort of. Funny how my companions on a drinking bender were bartenders who'd quit drinking. It was like I was getting absolution for drinking while I drank.

A lovely, pale-eyed blonde with shimmering hair appeared suddenly at Skipper's side. It made my night when she smiled at me. She couldn't have been more than twenty. Mick looked at me incredulously when she left with her order.

"Where do they get these women?"

"Ken screens them," Skipper told him. Ken owned the place.

"Ken, meet Barbie," Mick said laughing.

"Her name is Eden," said Skipper.

"It just gets better," said Mick.

After a while like that Mick and I headed out and looked in on Fat City. Nothing much going on there; the bartender wasn't in yet. Whitey's was almost next door. Reading the poster from the night before we saw that the Thumbheads had played the night before. Mick and I had become fans. They couldn't play, they couldn't sing. But we liked their cynical songs abusing their New Age groupies. Besides, the two lead Thumbheads, Bronco and Skank, were pearl divers at Fellini's.

Whitey's turned out to be a downer. The bartender was someone neither of us had seen before. He carried himself like a jock gone to seed, and he had the burned-out eyes of a stoner with a coke jones looking for a fight. He took his sweet time with our order, stiffing me with a double when I'd ordered a triple and throwing Mick a look of contempt when Mick ordered a spritzer. It was no fun on tour when you didn't know the bartender and he turned out to be a jerk.

"I give him a week," said Mick. "He just doesn't have the Whitey's vibe."

"Let's head back home," I said. "Plunkett's probably got some scalps he wants to show us."

"Yeah," said Mick, "and this guy is killing my bourbon-buzz flashback."

As we got up and moved towards the door, I saw Susan's Drew, dressed as usual for a funeral. We locked eyes. He smiled at me as the cat smiles at the canary. I said nothing. He said nothing. But something about that smile made me think of the bullet I'd dodged a couple hours ago outside the Bowers Library. Neither Mick nor I said a word on the short walk back to Fellini's. As we stood at the entrance, Mick rocked back.

"Shit, my ex-wife is in there."

I looked in and saw her. Mick's last wife was Chief's second. The ex and current husbands liked each other. Neither of them got on with her. I liked her myself.

"I'm out of here," said Mick.

"I'm not," I replied. We shook hands.

"I'm tending bar Friday," he said.

"I'll be here," I replied. I watched him walking up Second Street in the dark with a chipper, rolling gait. Thinking about Drew about Susan about Vandillingham, I decided I needed a drink. Plunkett was back at the bar, and he waved me in, as he cleared someone out of my stool.

"Sorry pal, you'll have to get up, that's Jack's stool" I heard him say as the door closed on the world outside.

17. Phonograph Blues

Beatrice got a phonograph
And it won't say a lonesome word
What evil have I done?
What evil has the poor girl heard?
Robert Johnson

Tuesday and Thursday came and went. No Vandillingham appeared at my classroom door at the conclusion of either class. Nor did he appear on the following Tuesday. I was beginning to think that events had been decided in my favor on the astral plane. Thursday, March 14, was the last day of classes before spring break. Only a handful of the usual handful trudged dutifully into class that morning. I had just begun to speak when there was a stentorian knock at the door and the academic secretary who had handed me the box of accumulated mail two weeks before entered without invitation. I had since learned that she was Vandillingham's personal secretary.

"How are your teeth, Mr. Shock?" she asked, smiling nonbenevolently.

"Teeth?" I asked. Wheels turned in the sandbox. The phantom root canal. "Ah, teeth," I said.

"No dental appointment today?" she asked, winking at my students as if they were in on the joke.

She walked over to the podium and attempted to place an envelope in my hand.

"Mr. Vandillingham said you were to read this letter in my presence and that I was not to leave until you had acknowledged it with a reply," she said.

So I took the envelope from her and ripped it in half as I fed deep, deep upon her peerless eyes. Then, still smiling, I ripped the two pieces in half again. I did that until there was nothing left to rip. Then I tossed the pieces into the air like confetti and let them fall.

"Pick them up!" she commanded; the greatness of Vandillingham put steel into her voice.

"You pick them up," I answered. "Take them to Mr. V.D. and tell him to stick them where the moon don't shine."

She stood there blushing with indignation. Even her moles turned red.

"Mr. Van — "

"Get out of here, you toady," I cut in. "Tell Vandillingham to hop up my ass."

The effect on the handful of the handful was galvanizing. For the first time since the semester had begun, I had their complete attention. A pretty girl in the front row whose name I didn't know and whose reaction to me seemed to oscillate between a reluctant crush and full blown disapproval, laughed out loud. And that laugh sent Vandillingham's secretary into full retreat. She backed away, turned, and walked quickly out of the door she'd left half open. With that the class broke into spontaneous applause. This I acknowledged only with a sad shake of my head and a downward glance at what I laughingly called my "lecture notes." Flannery Connor was the only thing written on every page, poor thing. I showed her the same mercy I had showed Bernie's secretary, doing justice to neither. The class actually seemed to pay attention, despite my usual lackluster droning performance. At the end, several students wished me a "fun" spring break; one of them actually used the word "awesome." How easy to be cool. Cruelty to Bernie's secretary had made me their hero.

The great man had stationed himself at the center of the hallway just outside the door, staring stonily as the students flowed past him, left and right. His face was twitching like a cat with a dust bunny on one of its whiskers. I had moved to the chair stationed behind the square wooden desk on the dais, the fortress from which I sent forth my bolts of wisdom. Waiting for Bernie, I put my boots up and striking a match on the edge of my left heel, lit a cigarette. Streams of acrid Turkish tobacco smoke scented the air with a smell like burning athletic socks.

"How dare you use obscenity! How dare you insult Dottie in front of your class!" he shouted as he walked towards me.

I blew a couple of smoke rings and watched them dissipate, then I said, "You have no right to inflict your vendetta on my students, Vandillingham. I'm pretty sure the Dean will back me up on that point."

"We'll see about that," Bernie snorted. He stepped onto the dais and slapped one of those official greenish envelopes on the desk.

"Read this, now!" he said.

"What happened to civility? What happened to 'Read this now', Professor Shock?" I asked, picking up the envelope.

I took my own sweet time. First I extracted from my pocket the old man's bakelite-handled Iroquois three blader, the one he'd carried in his flight jacket during a couple hundred missions in WWII. Next I opened the longest blade, slit the envelope, folded the knife using the edge of the desk top, took a deep puff on the Camel stuck to the corner of my mouth, and exhaled compendiously, narrowing my eyes to ward off the smoke. Then I put the knife back in my pocket and pulled the letter by its northeast corner from the

98

envelope, letting it drop to the floor beside the scattered pieces of the first letter. I shook the letter open and moved it closer to my face, making a great show of finding the exactly correct range for my eyes to engage its print. Then I began to pretend to read it, moving my lips to shape make believe words, wincing in pretended astonishment, taking a long time to let Old Bernie simmer in his juices.

I couldn't help noticing as I skimmed, however, that once again my presence was required in the Bowers Library and that the "court date" had been set for 9 o'clock on the morning of the 15th, less than twenty-four hours from now.

I was not sure yet whether I would show up, but I had the distinct impression that if I didn't, this time some bureaucratic line in the sand would be crossed and that my head would be on the block beside a keen axe before the semester's end.

"OK," I said, crumpling up the letter and tossing it into the bleachers.

"I'm warning you, Shock, — "

"You're not warning me, Bernie. You are boring me."

With that I swung my legs onto the floor and turned my back to him, pretending to scrutinize my phantom lecture notes.

When I turned around, he was gone. I decided to kill time waiting for my 3:30 class by ambling down to the Corner for lunch. I ordered three Millers at the Virginian with some peanut appetizers. As I started up the hill to McGregor Hall, I thought I caught sight of Vandillingham disappearing around the corner of one of the alleys between the West Range and the Lawn with a slinky blonde in heels and an ankle length black cashmere coat. I could almost smell her perfume. Wheeling my head around, I expected to see but didn't her pink BMW in one of the Range parking lots.

Why, I asked myself, would Bernard Vandillingham, a man who had no practical use for womankind, and none at all for a mantrap like Donna, have arranged a meeting today with her on University grounds? Why not just call her up at the real estate office, for example? It had something to do with the burning at the stake of Jack Shock; you could depend on that.

Racking my brains, I tried to recall some moment of indiscretion with Susan that Donna might present as "evidence" of a sexual encounter before her graduation. I could remember nothing. But then to tell the truth, my brain was a sieve. Two years of hollow leg, suicidal drinking had come and gone since those days and, hell, maybe something had happened. I took refuge once again in my own private Blackstone: Hide! And if they find you, lie. In the present case, a regular post modern witch hunt, I might even be the only one telling the truth.

I got back to my office, sat down, lit a cigarette. The place looked like a train wreck. Beer cans, empty Jim Beam bottles of every size from airline mini-fifths to half gallons lined the bookshelves. I don't mean to imply that there was an order in their arrangement. Why had I kept them at all? Trophies? Merit Badges? Tomorrow's collectibles? Inertia?

As I sat there smoking, the phone rang. I never got calls in that office. Never. The last call I remembered was from Sam while I was reading the old man's letter. I winced at the memory. I let the phone ring on. And it rang and it rang like the crying of an inconsolable child. Maybe someone knew I was holed up in here. Gingerly, I lifted the phone off the receiver.

"Jack," she said. It was Sam.

"I can't believe it's you," I said.

"I know," she said.

"What do you know?" I asked.

"I know you love me," she said.

And she hung up. After I hung up, I sat there for a long time, trying not to think of her. What I needed was a drink.

I got up and walked down to the room where I taught my graduate class and wrote "Class Cancelled" on the blackboard, signing my name. Then I walked to the parking lot, fired up the Continental, and drove to Fellini's to prepare for my court date.

It was still light when I shouldered through the door. Chief MacGruder, dressed like the *Casablanca* Bogart in a white tuxedo, stood beside the cash register speaking to a prosperous looking couple.

"Drinks? Dinner? That sort of thing?"

He and I exchanged nods as he said these very words, words I had heard him say a hundred times just since I'd been back from C.A.

Tending bar tonight was Fluffy, my idea of a feast for the eyes. As soon as she saw me, God bless her heart, she picked up the silvery cocktail shaker and filled it with ice. She extracted the bottle of Jim Beam with Jack Shock written on it, poured five neat shots into the shaker, shook it ten times, and then poured the result into a highball glass. I threw it down in one long swallow. Before I'd finished it, on the bar before me was a glass of ice water. I drank that down too.

"Fluffy, you are the fastest bartender in this town. And the best."

"The best at what, Jack?"

"At whatever."

She gave me a straight look.

"I don't think you've seen me at my actual best, Jack."

"The night is young, Fluff. The night is young."

Fluffy, a Tri Delt in former days, was now on the twelve-year-plan at the University. During the time I'd known her, she seemed to have bypassed pretty and gone directly to sex kitten. She was anything but fluffy.

She walked over to Chief who was talking to Mick who'd been discussing Schopenhauer with Victor.

"He had me with his first sentence," Mick was saying. "'The World is my idea.'"

"I like that," said Victor. "'The World is *my* idea ...'"

"As long as it isn't Chief's idea" Fluffy said blandly. "Chief thinks a party is sixteen horny squaws and one chief." She was looking at her nails as she said this.

"Fluff, you are such a liar!" Chief said laughing.

"Why, Chief, you've got the biggest dick I've ever seen." Fluffy looked up from her nails as she said this and batted her lashes, wide-eyed.

Everyone at that end of the bar except Fluffy laughed, no one louder than Chief. The laughter spread down the bar in a wave, sometimes with a word of explanation thrown in. It was the laughter of middle-aged men, smokers most of them, men who hadn't come to Fellini's to fight or fuck but to drink. A dry illusionless laughter like the rattle of musketry in an old war movie.

18. If I Had Possession Over the Judgement Day

If I had possession over the judgement day
The woman I'm loving wouldn't
Have no right to pray
Robert Johnson

At precisely nine o'clock the next morning I stumbled into the Bowers Library, uncombed, unshaven, unwashed, and dressed in the same clothing I'd worn the day before: a red-check wool shirt, blue jeans Sam had bought me, scuffed brown desert boots, heels rounded by two years in Central America; a beat-to-the-wide horsehide jacket. My hat, ten years old with a sweat ring above the ribbon, stayed on my head.

I felt as rough as — rougher — than I must have looked. It had been a long night of after hours drinking first at the Standard, then the upstairs room at Whitey's and finally at Fellini's. Along the way, Eden, the Barbie from the Standard and I had developed sentimental feelings for one another. I distinctly remembered watching her and another naked goddess dancing on Slab, the biggest table in the house. As she reached her arms out to me, the flesh was willing, but my heart belonged to another. At eight o'clock I awoke alone on Slab, considerably disarranged, when Fortune Ragland clanged in. Coffee-colored with hazel eyes that had seen it all, he eked out his railroad pension by cleaning up the messes of Fellini's-nights-before. He gave me coffee with a shot of bourbon to settle my shakes and a piece of last night's cheesecake to settle my gut.

So now I sat here, grubby but unbowed. And there they sat at the far end of twenty feet of dingy library rug, the Mild Bunch, my accusers and my judges. My stronghold, a twin to the desk in my Chesnutts of Dixie class; theirs, an oak table for five.

On the extreme left I was glad to see Edgar Levine, my professor of Shakespeare from undergraduate days. Later someone said he had insisted on being present, God bless him. Beside Edgar sat a known quantity, Morton Battlestation, a champion of Fielding, and as tolerant of human frailty in another as in himself. I was glad to see him too.

On the extreme right sat Vandillingham, another known quantity, his nose glowing as if it had been waxed and his face a host to tics and twitches fed by neuroses. To his right I saw Pat Beine, no friend to Jack Shock, who surveyed my sorry presence with a look of dogged unforgiveness.

At the center of the table sat El Importante, he whom Bill Smalls had socked in the snout when I ducked at the Smalls Thing. I now knew him as Roderigo Alhambra, recently and expensively imported from the Ivied northeast to reshape the department in his own image as a post modern icon. His list of publications exceeded the combined bibliographies of everyone else in the room, my lackluster self included. Looking at him, I could not tell whether he would play Judge Roy Bean to my incorrigible horse thief or Solomon the wise to my baby's snatcher. Soon enough, I reckoned, all would be revealed.

"Mr. Shock," said Alhambra. "How are you this morning?" He spoke slowly and sonorously without a trace of irony, like one who relishes nothing so much as the music of his own voice, enhanced by a hint of a middle European accent, whether actual or affected who could say? The accent went well with his persona: he was dressed in a dark — probably tailored — Italian suit, a blue silk shirt and a silver tie of the same material. His shoes alone had probably cost more than all the clothes everyone else had on put together in Bowers that day.

"As well as can be expected," I answered in a voice colored by recent saturations of bourbon and tobacco.

Levine and Battlestation smiled. Bernie and Beine scowled. Alhambra's face showed nothing at all except conviction in his own greatness.

"We are here, Mr. Shock — Jack — to examine you on two charges ..." At this point I confess I cast my brain adrift and ceased listening. I do remember "sexual relations with an undergraduate woman, your student ..." and towards the end Alhambra turning to Bernie with the phrase "I wonder if we may begin with the lesser charge since it is so much more nebulous ..."

"As you wish, Roderigo," said Bernie with strident affability.

"May I ask a question?" I intruded.

El Importante turned and blinked at me as if he had not before thought of me as an actual participant in the proceedings.

"Certainly ...!" he said, drawing out the word by caressing every syllable, especially the first and the last.

"Who brought this charge?"

"Ahhhh ..." he replied.

"Because," I continued, though the "Ahhh" went on, "unless someone other than the persons present," I pointed with my face at Vandillingham, "has actually filed a complaint, a student for example?" I let my words hang there — "Then I'm pretty sure this charge is bogus."

"Here! Here!" said Edgar. God bless him.

"Ahhhh … Mr. … Ahh … Shock. Could you excuse us for a moment?" intoned Alhambra.

Beside himself, Vandillingham had popped up and perched himself on Alhambra's right shoulder. Beine, Battlestation and Levine leaned in. I heard some stage whispering.

"Gladly," I answered finally and irrelevantly to no one. This was my cue for a smoke. As I got to the door, Vandillingham called out, "He's getting away!"

"Don't worry. I'll be in my office, Bernie," I said, remembering the pint of Jim Beam in the desk drawer.

When I got there, however, I decided after all to forego my dose of painkiller. I was already drunk enough for a couple of ordinary drunks. Instead I decided to give my dear wife a call. I lit a cigarette while the phone rang.

"Hole-in-One Realty," I heard Hazel say. I had to put my hand over the receiver to stifle my guffaw.

"Have you by any chance changed your name? I mean your company's name?" I asked.

"Yes, we have," said Hazel. I could tell she recognized my voice. "Miss Prileau is not here at the moment."

"Alas, I was calling to speak with her."

"Is this Jack Shock?" she asked, slyly.

"It is, Hazel."

Obligingly, Hazel recited some digits that I recognized as the phone number at the cabin that I had never bothered to reconnect. For two years dear old Donna had been monitoring my phone calls. I dialed my number. At the precise moment I had decided to hang up, Donna's voice jolted me from my light bulb moment.

"Jack," she said, "Is that you?" It was I said. Damn the woman. How did she know? Had I coughed? Mumbled?

"Donna, did I see you yesterday on grounds with Bernie?"

"Who is Bernie?"

"The same Bernie you told I was sleeping with Susan two years ago."

"Who is Susan?" she asked.

"The Susan you gave advice to about what to expect by way of compensation for sleeping with a professor."

"Oh, that Susan," she went on. "Yes. I was on grounds yesterday. Bernie? Yes, Bernie is looking for a house — "

"A Hole in One?" I broke in. "Donna, spare me your fictions. I just want to know if you are in some way a part of the 'Exterminate Jack Shock' festivities today in Bowers."

"Bowers?" she said. "Where's Bowers?"

"Good-bye Donna," I said. I hung up.

One down. One to go. The next number I had to get from the University operator. Susan answered on the second ring.

"Hello?" She did not sound good.

"Susan." I was sure she recognized my voice although all she said was: "This is she."

"Yes it is," I said.

"Jack." Her voice was faint, cryptic.

"Susan, I have to ask you something."

"Yes?" Very faint.

"Are you part of Vandillingham's Trial of the Century?"

She knew what I meant all right. I could tell by the audible intake of her breath.

"I have been asked to come."

"When?"

"After lunch." Faint again.

"I can't wait to hear what you have to say." And I hung up.

It now seemed possible that Susan had gone over to the dark side. Oh well. A while later I heard a knock at the door.

"Yes," I said.

"They are waiting for you." It was Dottie. I said nothing. I heard her footsteps in the hall. I put out my smoke. In a bare minute I had resumed my seat at the dock.

"Ahhhhh," said Roderigo. Here we go again, I thought.

"We have decided for the present — uh — to omit consideration of the second charge. As you correctly have said — ahhh — this is a matter that requires a student complaint."

"As I think, does the first charge," I said braving the matter out.

"Hear! Hear!" said Edgar Levine, God bless the man.

There was a knock at the door. I saw the chastened face of Dottie, my scapegoat for Vandillingham the day before. I realized that I now regretted what I had said to her.

"I need to speak to Mr. Vandillingham, please," she said. And after a moment added, "And to Mr. Alhambra." And after another moment she added, "An urgent message."

"Right," I said. And I wondered which of the two the message was from. "I'll be outside," I said. "I need a cigarette."

At one o'clock I was again seated in Bowers, after a three beers and peanuts lunch at The Virginian. While the Mild Bunch chewed over the call, Dottie had come out to tell me that the trial, "the meeting," she called it, had been delayed. I apologized, after a fashion, for our contretemps of the day before, and she, after a fashion, accepted. We were not friends and likely never would be. But she was not the enemy. The real enemy was the fellow I avoided the sight of in the mirror every time I chose that barstool at Fellini's.

Just outside the hall I heard the thin sharp staccato tap of high heels. No woman who worked in MacGregor ever wore them there. But I knew somebody who wore them, even in bed.

19. From Four Til Late

From four til late
She sot with a no good bunch and clowned,
She didn't do nothing
But tear a good man's reputation down.

Robert Johnson

Whenever Donna entered a room she had already calculated the impression she would make. I remembered watching twelve years before the Tri Delt Sea parting for the golden girl in a white dress with sun-bleached hair and sunburnt skin. Every eye turned to her, desire or envy stamped on every face, not excepting my own.

Desire was the last thing I felt as I processed her entrance today. But she had made damn sure she looked good. Her suit of gray gabardine was cut a little short in the leg and tight in the bust for business attire. The dark red sweater was from Prague. The pearls from her grandmother. Her long legs and full breasts I remembered well, though I had not seen her since the night she'd thrown the lit cigarette at my face. No doubt she had a hotter fire in mind for me today.

To the uninitiated, Donna's stop at my desk conveyed sympathy for her fallen husband. She seized both my hands, looking me in the eyes with all the sympathy of a deep sea crustacean. All but spoken between us were the words "There you are, you stupid bastard" and "Hello there, you lying bitch." Her downcast eyes twinkling with crocodile tears, Donna glided on to the Mild Bunch. Beginning with Edgar, she shook hands with each of them except for Bernie with whom she exchanged a chaste, arms-length "hug." It was quite a performance. At the end of it, she took her seat in a plush chair about ten feet closer to Vandillingham than it was to me as he gazed on her as if she were the new oracle of the post modern gospel.

Standing beside his seat, Bernie launched into a fictional account of Donna's life in Charlottesville as my wife and chief victim. He ignored her many affairs including the one with Bill Smalls, Bill being since the Smalls Thing, little more than a walking corpse as far as the department was concerned. On the other hand, my affair with Susan Monteith became in Bernie's narrative but one link in the daisy chain of lust which I had inflicted on undergraduate womankind. As it went on I cast myself adrift in the wide sargasso sea of my mind; eyes downcast, I hummed inaudibly blocking out everything except the odd phrase.

Then a query from Morton Battlestation interrupted Bernie's jeremiad and called me back to the proceedings. There he sat, his left arm cocked at the elbow, his left hand cradling his very large, very round, very pink head crowned by sheaf of silver hair. His expression declared an intolerance for blather, something Bernie possessed in bottomless supply. Morton was saying "So when did Jack first actually teach Miss - ah - I'm sorry," he glanced down at his notes "Miz Monteith"?

Frustrated by his inability to get a word in edgewise, Alhambra began chanting or stuttering — it was hard to tell which — the sound "Uh-uh-uh ..." until he ceased, having discovered, no doubt, he had nothing to say.

"I believe it was spring 1987," Bernie answered after a pause.

"It was the fall of 1986," I said. Morton kept his eyes on me as he went on, "So did a ... liaison? — you admit to one eventually, right, Jack?" Morton continued as I nodded, "Ah, did a sexual relationship begin during or as a result of that class?"

"No," I answered.

"And the class was . . . ah, ENTC 312? ENAM 312?"

"Greatest Hits of the Twentieth Century," I replied.

"So ... ENTC 312. And how many students in the class?"

"I don't know ... a hundred sixty, a hundred eighty? Something like that.

"Did any sort of, ah, relationship — I don't mean an affair — begin then?" Morton asked.

"Did it?" Bernie interjected looking at Donna.

"Yes" from Donna.

"No" from Jack Shock.

"What evidence," Morton was looking at Donna steadily as he spoke, "is there that Jack was in actual fact anything to, ah, Susan Monteith other than her teacher in 1986?"

"None," I said under my breath.

"I saw them together," Donna said, her chin lifted, her nose wrinkled. To me these tics were a sure tell that Donna was lying.

"Where?" I broke in. "Doing what? Crossing the street in opposite directions?"

"Where, Donna?" Vandillingham's voice was flute-like, soothing, cajoling. She smiled generously at her deliverer.

108

"Ah ... Uh ... Uh ..." Alhambra interjected. "If no one objects, uh ... I would like ...," he looked at each participant in turn, "to put the question to Donna, myself." Then he repeated, though it took him much longer, the exact words that Vandillingham had just spoken.

Jack Shock, for one, was all ears. What factoid would Donna, a practiced but inept liar supply to seal her husband's fate?

"I caught them in our bed together," she said. Succinct and monolithic, this lie stopped the Mild Bunch in their tracks. But not Jack Shock.

"Donna," I said, "you must be confusing your own couplings with mine." I looked at my judges. "I have never" — I almost said the f-word — "copulated with anyone in our bed except for you." I looked at her. "I never had sex with Susan until you "eloped" with Bill Smalls." I wanted that fact on the record, if in fact there was a record.

The eyes of the Mild Bunch shifted from Jack to Donna. One of us at least, after all, had to be a liar.

"In our bed!" Donna repeated boldly lifting her chin and staring resolutely at Bernie.

It was Edgar Levine who broke the silence with an observation that was as obvious as it was irrefutable: "Given the contradiction between the recollections of Donna and Jack, there is no point in going on until we hear from Susan Monteith."

Morton Battlestation and Jack Shock shook their heads in agreement.

"And I move," Edgar continued, "that we adjourn until she ..."

"One minute," Vandillingham interjected, "I wonder, Donna, could you please elaborate on your memory of that day ... in bed."

"That's right, Donna," Jack Shock broke in, "Were Susan and I copulating in the tried-and-true missionary position, or were we entangled in something more exotic?"

"I agree with Edgar," broke in Battlestation, diplomatically. "It's pointless to encourage these colorful ... uh evocations." We need to hear from Susan Monteith."

"I agree," said Roderigo cryptically.

"With whom?" asked Edgar, looking at Alhambra who in turn looked puzzled.

"With whom?" Alhambra repeated.

"Agree with Bernie or with Edgar?" I interrupted.

"With Edgar *and* Bernie," Alhambra answered, as if no other answer were possible. Puzzlement marked the faces of the Mild Bunch, except of course, the face of Roderigo Alhambra, post modern icon. Jack Shock, for his part, considered pointing out the deficiencies of El Importante's pronouncement but wisely he decided not to do so.

"So, Donna," Vandillingham resumed, how long did your husband's affair with the undergraduate Susan Monteith last? Weeks? Months?

"Decades?" From Jack Shock.

"I have something to say," Pat Beine was standing, her voice shaking. "I am *offended* by the lack of gravitas that this enquiry has taken on." She looked at each of her colleagues, then at Donna, and finally at Jack Shock. Seeing her eyes, Jack flinched, awaiting the blast.

"I am particularly offended by the demeanor and the commentary of this man." Here she pointed at Jack Shock; the gray dumpling herself trembled from chin to foot.

"A young woman has been violated — violated! Violated by a professor from this department ..."

Once again I dropped my eyes and ceased listening; humming inaudibly I began drifting down the river Ganga towards lotus land, as I recalled the night when lovely Susan and lonely Jack Shock had first made love.

It was a Tuesday night, the week of graduation, Susan had just begun working at Fellini's. At closing time, with a look I could not then interpret, Plunkett sent me upstairs with a bottle of wine. It was dark going up the stairs, lit only by a skylight on a moonless, starry night. It was darker when I got up there. An aura of stardust outlined a form. It was Susan stepping out of her dress, and as my eyes adapted to the dark, I could see she had nothing on underneath it.

"Jack," she whispered, as she drew me to Queen, the only table in the loft. "Make love to me, Jack, make love to me on Queen."

Later, when I discussed my misgivings with Mick Reardon about my affair with a student, he looked at me incredulously.

"Who are *you* to deny *her* what *she* wants?

A horn sounded through the pleasant fog of this memory. It was the outraged voice of Bernard Vandillingham.

"Look at him!" he was pointing at me. "The insensitive son of a bitch is asleep! He is actually asleep!"

"No, Bernie," I said, but for no ears but my own. "I just wish I was." And I opened my eyes.

"What do you have to say for yourself, Shock?" he demanded.

"I say this. Unless you can produce Susan Monteith, I am going to walk out of this farce. I am going to drive back to Nelson County and pour myself a stiff belt of bullshit-solvent." I cleared my throat and spat into the trashcan beside the desk where I sat.

Time had stopped. This was clearly Jack's exit line.

Given the lack of sleep and the super-abundance of alcohol my poor body had to reckon with up to that moment, I felt rather proud of myself for getting it all out, and I mean the words, more than the phlegm. I stood up to leave.

"Wait!" Bernie shouted. "He's going to walk out!"

"Calm down, Bernie. Calm down." It was Edgar. "And, Roderigo, forgive me. I must speak. An unproven accusation of sexual harassment has ruined more than one colleague." He looked at all present meaningfully.

"And after all, each of us perhaps has found himself or herself," he looked at Pat Beine placatingly, "involved with students in a friendship where the question "Am I going too far?" has come up. Even you, Bernie."

Bernie turned crimson. Almost imperceptibly, he was trembling.

Edgar moved on: "I for one second Jack's opinion that this proceeding is a farce, tainted by ad hominem attacks."

"And hypocrisy," Morton Battlestation added; at least two other heads nodded in agreement.

"But," Morton continued, "Edgar, Jack, I want to ask Bernie a question that we all want answered."

"And uh uh uh uh ... what question is that?" I was so astounded that Alhambra had actually spoken a complete thought that I almost said "Well done, Roderigo!"

"The question is," Morton responded, "Where is Susan Monteith? Didn't Dottie tell Bernie that Susan promised to be here by three o'clock?"

All of us, Donna included, raised our eyes to the round face of time fixed to the eastern wall of Bowers Library. It was four minutes to three.

There came a knocking at the door; Dottie entered just as far as my desk.

"Susan Monteith is here," she said.

"Send her in," said Morton.

20. We Played It On The Sofa

We played it on the sofa
We played it on the wall
My needle has got rusty
and it will not play at all.

Robert Johnson

Wide-eyed and appalled, like someone who stumbles into a strobe lit room from the dark, Susan Monteith stood for a moment at the door. She had chosen to appear in jeans and a grey turtleneck sweater, the uniform of a graduate student that winter. Her short chestnut hair was drawn back in a careless twist. She wore no jewelry at all. Her eyes were wary and resentful.

The first person she looked at was me. Reading her face, I knew I looked even worse than I felt. In her eyes I saw only kindness. She smiled and said faintly, "Hello, Jack."

Vandillingham's voice was already manhandling her in a proprietary way.

"Come in, Susan. Come over here. You'll be sitting by us."

Everyone at that end was standing except Donna. The faces of the Mild Bunch each wore some version of a tentative, uneasy smile. Donna's look was cool and appraising. As she was introduced to each of them, Susan hung back, keeping her distance. She shot a narrow-eyed glance at Donna before the golden girl nodded a perfunctory hello. A chair across from Donna was pointed out to her and Susan sat down on its edge as if she expected to spring up and escape at the earliest opportunity.

Immediately, Vandillingham moved that I be excluded from the library during Susan's testimony on the grounds that I might attempt to influence or intimidate her. I said nothing. The truth was I was pretty much done in. I had slept less than two hours after a night of kamikaze drinking, among other excesses. The levels of my blood sugar had now tumbled. I was actually hoping Bernie's motion would pass so I could lie down on the carpet at my feet and go to sleep.

The discussion that followed was predictable: Bernie and Beine on one side, Battlestation and Levine on the other, El Importante silent in his inscrutable magnificence. Susan raised her hand. "I wonder," she asked, "could we have some coffee, please?"

Everyone and everything stopped at once. "I'm sure we can have some brought in," Morton assured her.

"I'll go out and put some on — the secretaries have all gone home," said Edgar. "I have to call my wife and tell her we'll be here for a while."

"Thank you," said Susan, still coolly formal, "also …" she went on "may I say something about what you are about to vote on? I mean about whether Jack should be here when I answer your questions."

"By all means" said Alhambra rather succinctly for him.

"I think that Jack looks tired," Susan said softly. "I'm afraid he may not be well."

All eyes turned to Jack Shock slumped inelegantly in his chair.

"I'll be all right after I drink some coffee," I said very slowly." I'd like to get this finished. I don't want to sit through another day of this dreck. I'd rather proceed directly to the foregone conclusion."

"I think Jack should be here when I testify," Susan paused. "He has that right, I believe. I'm not intimidated by him," she smiled at me, "and I don't want to say anything about our former relationship unless he hears it." Again she paused. "I want you all to know that I did not come here …" Her voice had again grown faint; she took a deep breath and went on: "I am not here because I want to be here."

She looked at me as she said this. A feeling that I was not alone welled up in me. I had been wrong to think that Susan had sold me out for thirty pieces of silver, whether Vandillingham's coin or Donna's.

"I am here," she went on, "because Mr. Vandillingham insisted that I come. I'm taking his class —"

Vandillingham reacted with one of his bad smell expressions, fidgeting and moving his mouth.

"Are you implying that I have attempted to influence you?"

"I'm not implying it," she replied, "I'm saying it." She looked at him. "Because you have."

"This matter will be looked into," said Roderigo with astonishing economy. He continued, "Mr. Shock will stay." Then he turned to Morton and invited him to begin with Susan. Fingering his notes, Morton got on with it.

"I understand your concern for Mr. Shock and to some degree I share it," said Morton. "While we wait for coffee, I want to inform you that Jack has told us that you and he were intimate."

Susan colored. She raised her head. Her back straightened. She said nothing, but there was a hint of defiance in her silhouette.

Morton reacted. "I apologize for intruding on your private life. It's personally distasteful to me to ask you these questions …" He paused and looked up as Edgar reentered the room. He and Edgar exchanged a pregnant look, as Edgar resumed his seat.

"Susan, we've established that you took ENAM, no, ENTC 312 from Mr. Shock in the fall of 1986."

Susan reflected briefly and nodded, her eyes still wary.

"Did you know him before that class?"

"I did not."

"Did you become friendly … during or after that class?"

"I had a first year crush on him, but I never saw him, I mean, talked to him, 'went out' with him," she pantomimed the quotation marks with her fingers. "Isn't that what you are asking?"

"Yes," Morton smiled and went on. "That's exactly what I am asking."

"We weren't lovers until I was done with classes, at the end of my fourth year."

"Yes, that's very helpful," Morton said. He paused, made a note on his notes, looked up, and smiled at me, avoiding Donna, sullen since Susan had begun to speak. My dear wife's eyes were fixed on a spot about an inch above the chairman's head. Edgar and Morton consulted briefly in whispers and Edgar spoke:

"I believe, Roderigo, that we have detained Donna long enough …" Alhambra took his point and turned to Donna.

"We - uh - thank you - uh - uh - Donna for - uh - your help, and we will be contacting you - uh - soon." He nodded to each of the professoriat, except of course Jack Shock.

Donna stood up, shot Alhambra a contemptuous look, ignoring everyone, except Vandillingham. To him her smile was brief and glacial. The glance she sent me, on her way to the door, acknowledged that things had not gone well for the golden girl. But it also told me that she would make sure I got what I had coming for having failed to live up to her constantly changing and limitless expectations.

Fifteen minutes later after we had adjourned briefly for bad coffee and in my case three cigarettes and a good head soak in a sink of cold water, Susan's testimony resumed. The baton had passed to Pat Beine, who, furious at the fact that Susan had had her way with me rather than vice versa, stared stonily into the middle distance and kept her own counsel. It now passed to Vandillingham, who after listening to Susan's heavily censored version of our first encounter on Queen, honed in on the date of our coupling four days before Susan's graduation. "So you were still an undergraduate" Vandillingham exalted. "Technically, I guess," Susan returned.

Vandillingham had found the Holy Grail. He exacted from both Susan and Jack acknowledgement of that date. Once Susan had graduated, I moved in with her, which in our case meant I slept at her house on Altamont Street any night I came into town. To the University, the sequel meant nothing. It was that one night on Queen that gave Vandillingham the hope that he could send me tumbling headlong into hell. Or at least get me fired. Edgar and Morton each dissented, saying that at worst Susan, in Morton's phrase, was "in limbo" because as Edgar put it, "Jack had not taught her since first year" and never had pursued a relationship with her. With that, after some procedural blah-blah-blah, everyone went home.

But not Jack. I found myself alone in the sterile, Bartleby-dead-wall-space of MacGregor Hall, overcome by a fatigue so profound that I believed if I sat down I would fall into a sleep that I would never wake up from. Very slowly, I forced my way through the doors of Sing Sing. It seemed like an hour before the Continental came into view.

Susan had fled MacGregor immediately after the last blah-blah-blah was spoken, so I was surprised to find her waiting for me beside my car. She was shivering there with her arms folded across her breasts watching me steadily as I stumbled, fell, got up, and stumbled again, this time without falling. I was worse off than if I'd been drinking all day. She put her arm around me and shunted me into the back seat where I collapsed on a bed of all the mail I'd providentially decided not to read for the last three months. I was asleep before I landed. After that I remember nothing of the next twelve hours.

She drove me home, not to mine but hers. I awoke the next morning in her bed alone, my clothes washed, warm, and folded on the chair beside me. I raised my head to look out the window at the day, and seeing the rain, fell back, and was asleep as soon as my head hit the pillow.

I awoke again in the afternoon; my clothes on the chair were cool to the touch. Now I could hear the rain splattering against the window glass. Again, I fell asleep. When I awoke for the third and final time, the rain had stopped, and the sky was dark. I got up and showered, cleaned up, and using Susan's razor shaved my neck and cheeks. There was no one else in the house. Out of the living room window I could see the Continental, wet from the rain gleaming in the lights of Altamont Street where Susan had lived as long as I had known her. It was barely a hundred yards from her house to Fellini's. My mind was on my autographed bottle of Jim Beam when I found the note on the kitchen table written in Susan's graceful, flowing hand.

Dear Jack,

I'm sorry I hijacked you last night. I just couldn't let you drive home. I was afraid you'd wreck your car and hurt yourself. Drew helped me get you into bed. He said you smelled like a cross between a distillery and a tobacco barn.

I washed your clothes this morning. I didn't think you'd mind.

I'm sorry about my participation in the Bowers Thing yesterday. Really, everyone was pretty nice except for Mr. Vandillingham. You were right about him. I think he really does hate you. I'm sorry about that night at Fellini's, not about the night itself, but about your getting into trouble for it. Don't worry about what Vandillingham will do to me in the course. I've decided that graduate school in English is not for me. Most of my courses are more about the professors' egos than about the literature. But you know that already. I think I stayed with it this long just hoping to see you again.

I'm worried about you, Jack. The way you drink, everyone talks about it. The smoking is almost worse. You drink and smoke more than anyone I've ever known. You need to stop or at least cut down. The life you're leading, you can't lead long.

I can tell that underneath it all you're so unhappy. I used to think, back when we were lovers, that it was your wife. But I don't know. I think that you are lonely and proud and you'll always be that way. But the drinking makes it worse.

If you love that girl in Washington, the one you told me about (It isn't Sam, is it?), find her, tell her what you feel. Even if it doesn't work out, maybe if you just talk to her, it will make you stop doing the awful things you do to yourself to keep from feeling the pain.

I'm sorry for this rambling amateur analyst's letter. I'm sure you can tell that I still care about you. There is nothing bad in me towards you. I know you are a good man, Jack, just a very sad one.

Love,
Susan

P.S. Help yourself to anything you want. Yes, you can use my razor. I won't be back until seven. If you are still here, I'll make you something to eat.

As I read Susan's letter, I felt as though all of it were true, almost as if it were a letter I would have written myself if I'd actually cared enough about myself to write it. All that I tried to hide from was on that page. I had become the son of a bitch's son of a bitch. The little wars with Vandillingham and Donna, needling him, needling her, were just diversions. The real thing was waiting for me on Capitol Hill.

Just thinking about going up there made me want to drink til I was blotto. A hundred yards away was Fellini's, where they kept a bottle in the cooler with Jack written on it. Where they never asked you why. I was shaking like the wind chime on Susan's porch this cold wet windy night in March.

Somehow I had to find the nerve not to get blotto tonight. I had to drive up there, I had to find Sam, and I had to tell her about the letter. I believed I had to do all that if I wanted to ever live in my own skin again. If I ever wanted to get out of these blues alive.

I don't know where I got the strength to walk out to the Continental, but I did it. When I got behind the wheel, I did what I always did first thing. I reached under the seat and pulled out the pint bottle I kept there for emergencies. For maintenance, really. This time, for the first time, I opened the door and set the bottle upright in the grass beside the curb. Then I shut the door, turned the key in the ignition, and put the Continental into Drive. I drove off slowly, like a man who has a long way to go, to get someplace he isn't sure he can find again.

21. Steady Rolling Man

I'm the man who rolls

When icicles on the trees ...

Robert Johnson

The afternoon rain had glazed the highway in black ice and along it the oaks and poplars shone in my headlights like glass skeletons of trees picked clean by the wind and snow. Not a headlight did I see. At the turnoff to Banco a grey fox bolted across the road. I never thought to hit my brakes, but he made it by the skin of his teeth. I envied him his luck. In the moonlight the gleaming tin of a barnyard roof was another talisman, cryptic in its augury, the only light in all that blackness. As if drawn by the magnet of Polaris, the Lincoln glided on alone, north towards Washington.

Just past Culpeper, I stopped for gas. I washed down some Nabs with an RC Cola, staring as I drank at a six-pack of Rolling Rock longnecks in the icebox. It would have taken all six of them to slake my thirst and even then I knew my hand would not have been still.

"Care for a drink of white liquor?" said a voice. I turned to a wizened brown apple-faced man in clean faded bib overalls. "You look like it might could do you some good," he said.

He was right, depending how you defined good. My scalp prickled and the back of my neck had a hump in it the size of a softball. I looked so hard at the plastic Pepsi bottle he held out to me that he unscrewed the cap. I could smell the applejack a foot away.

"I'd best not," I said. "But I thank you."

Regret dogged my steps back to the car. I knew if I had drank my fill, I'd already be heading back to Charlottesville.

An hour later crossing the George Washington, I glimpsed the Potomac running east, tar black. I pulled over just past the Lincoln Memorial. The tremor in my hand was so bad I burnt my beard trying to light a cigarette. Again I almost turned back, for I told myself it was too late. Probably, she wasn't even home. And I felt exhausted already, as if I had swam all the way to Washington in a deep cold sea and then at the last could not find the strength to stumble the few yards left to shore. But I knew I had to go on, for as Susan had rightly said, the life I was leading I couldn't live long. Besides I could always go back to it and drink myself to death. I knew that if I didn't go forward, I would not have it in me to come as far as I had already come. Not

118

again. I knew too that if Sam were home, I would be looking her in the eye in less time than I had already spent smoking the cigarette now burning in the corner of my mouth. After a while I tossed the butt out the window, turned the key in the ignition, and drove on.

Just after eight o'clock, I drove up the General's street. The porch light was on beside the big red door. I fell out of the car when the door opened and staggered the first few steps, feeling pretty bad. I had to touch the ground with my right hand to keep from tumbling on my face. I squatted, looking back at the Continental, trying to believe there was still a pint of Jim Beam lying on the backseat floorboard, covered by letters, some of them dating back to the years I was in Central America. I shivered from my boots to my jaws, not from cold, though there was a frost in the air, but from the longing for a drink and from the nausea that I believed was the beginnings of the DTs. My head was throbbing and the muscles of my back were knotted up like whipcord. I had just launched myself back towards the car when I heard the door open behind me, groaning on its hinges like the weight of the world was behind it.

"Jack," I heard her say. "Is that you?"

I turned, rose up slowly, tottering, straightened my shoulders and took my hat off, ashamed.

"Sam," was all I said. She was so beautiful in the glimpse I'd had of her that I couldn't bring myself to look at her again. I didn't have the right. And damn me if the water wasn't falling again from my eyes on the crown of my grey felt hat.

"Come in," she said. I didn't move.

"Come in," she said again. She was dressed in her red tartan robe and her feet were bare. I still couldn't move. She walked out to me and touched my shoulder gently.

"Come in, Jack," she said softly. "I've built a fire."

I followed her in. The house pretty much looked as it always had. It wasn't tidy and it wasn't messy. I followed her to the den, where a fire crackled. I could see she had been sitting in the dark in one of the big wing chairs on either side of the hearth. I took my seat in the one across from her.

For a while neither of us said anything. I stared into the fire as a refuge from thought. Sam had her bare feet on the hearth. I noticed as I often had before that her second toe was longer than the big one and that her foot had a high arch.

"Look at me, Jack," she said softly. "Look at me." I looked at her. Her eyes glittered in the light from the hearth.

"I've been thinking about you," she said.

I nodded. "Me too," I said. "I mean, I've been thinking about you." My voice was awkward and stumbling, a lot like my walking. I was shaking all over like a Waring blender.

"I know," she said.

"I …" That's all I could get out. I felt I had to go on.

"I had to see you," I said.

"I know," she said.

"How do you know that?" I asked.

"Because I know you love me, Jack," she said. "I told you that already."

"I don't deny it," I said.

"Your face, Jack. You've never been able to hide anything you felt."

"Not from you, I guess. But I have been hiding something. That's why I'm here."

"I know that too," she said.

"What do you know?" I asked. "How do you know?"

"I know why you sent me away and why you came back tonight."

"No you don't. You can't."

"But I do," she said quietly. She looked at me, her eyes brimming. Then she got up and went to the General's desk. She opened it. Her hand found what it sought at once, even in the dark room lit only by the red glow of the fire. She had an envelope in her hand and when she came back she put it in mine. For a moment when my hand felt the touch of hers, it quit trembling. She touched my face very gently.

"You look tired, Jack."

"I look worse."

"You look sad," she said. Then she walked out of the room, leaving me with the envelope. I heard cabinets opening, clanging pots, kitchen noises. I opened the envelope and held it towards the fire to read by its light. It was almost a copy of the letter that the General had sent to me, except that it was addressed to her and there was nothing in it about probity. I couldn't swear to it but I was pretty sure it was dated the same day as the letter to me. I put it back in the envelope and lay it on her chair. Then I stared into the fire, trying for once not to let my mind vault ahead of what I felt.

Soon enough Sam came back with a tray and two mugs. She'd made cocoa. She looked at the letter on the chair. Then she set the tray on the hearth, picked up the letter, and put it back in the General's desk.

When she came back she sat stretched out on the hearth between the two wing chairs with her feet alongside mine. She handed me the chipped mug with a Model T on it, mine since childhood. Hers had a white crouching tiger. She looked into the fire and for a long time neither of us said anything.

"When did you know?" she asked.

"The night I saw you last. The first night I came back to the cabin … I'm sorry I handled it the way I did."

"It broke my heart," she said, looking towards the dark window behind me.

"It broke mine too," I said. In profile her face was pink from the glow of the fire.

"I know," she said.

"You know," I said softly. She looked up at me.

"I'm not sorry about us. I'm not sorry about any of it. I wanted it too."

I said nothing.

"Are you?"

"I wish I'd stayed in Guatemala. Nobody complicated things by giving a damn about me."

"That's no way to live, Jack," she looked at me sadly.

"I don't say it is," I said. "Sometimes life ain't all it's cracked up to be."

"Yes, it is," she said earnestly. "It's not easy sometimes, but you've got to keep your nerve up."

"You're right. It takes nerve to live in this world."

"Don't make fun of me," she said, but she was smiling.

"I'm not laughing," I said. "McFate may be laughing but I'm not."

"You and your McFate. Where did you get that from, anyway? Faulkner?"

"Nabokov," I said.

"Vladimir," she said. "The General liked him too."

"He liked his translation of *that*." I pointed to the volume of *A Hero of Our Time*. Then I got up and pulled the book from the shelf. I sat down and held it out to her. She took it, looked it over, and put it to one side. That meant she would read it whenever she finished what she was in the middle of reading now.

"He didn't like *Lolita*," I said. "That's where McFate comes from."

"What does it mean?" she asked.

I didn't want to sound like a college professor, not to her, not that I was much of one. Like Susan Monteith, I had pretty much had my fill of academic life. But I didn't feel like copping an attitude. Academia was no phonier than any other form of corporate self-aggrandizement. It hadn't always been the moral equivalent of Exxon and somewhere at someplace small it was probably still mostly about teaching. But while I'd been at the University it had almost always had the stink of snake oil.

"I think McFate means fate taking a human form in your own life. Even if Nabokov meant something else by it, that's how I use it myself."

"So am I your McFate?" she asked smiling up at me.

"No," I said. "You're the real thing."

"So I'm Fate with a capital F?"

"No," I answered. "You're not Fate, big F or little f."

I was telling her I loved her. She didn't look at me. Again we sat there for a long while looking at the fire.

"I want to talk about the letter," she said softly.

"Now the letter, that was McFate," I said.

"I don't believe it," she said.

"You don't believe what?"

"I don't believe that you and I are what the letter says we are."

"Brother and Sister."

"Yes, brother and sister. Or half brother and sister." She had pulled away from me completely and was kneeling on the floor with her back against her wing chair.

"I don't believe it," she said again.

"I'm listening," I said. "So what are we then?"

"You already know who your parents are," she said. "And I am my mother's daughter. But I am not your father's daughter."

"Is this your gut talking or is there more to it?"

"First of all," she said, "I don't think I look much like my mother. Remember, she was very fair."

She was right about Aunt Grace, and I thought I knew where she was going.

"And I look even less like *your* father."

"Stranger things have happened."

"Yes," she said. "Stranger things *have* happened. Now I want to show you something."

She got up and walked purposefully out of the room and up the stairs. I heard her above me in her bedroom. I watched the fire. The cocoa had made me a little sleepy. But the tremor was still there. I was not going to get drunk or to sleep tonight until all of this was thrashed out. And part of my shaking was the anticipation of whatever she had gone to find. A moment later she was standing beside me. In one hand she held a sepia colored envelope; in the other was a sheaf of old yellowed airmail letters with red and blue borders.

"Look at these," she said, handing me the envelope. It was filled with photographs. Most of them were small color photographs of a man and a woman. Sam turned on the reading lamp beside my chair.

"What are they?" I asked.

"The woman in the photographs is my mother." Looking at them in the light I could see that Sam was right. The pictures showed Aunt Grace, a young woman — younger than I was now — but the young man with her was neither my uncle nor my father. The way my aunt looked at the man in the picture — like he was the light of the world — and the pictures themselves — in one of them Aunt Grace's bare back was turned to the camera, as was her face, lit with a smile — all that made me think that the couple were lovers.

"Now look at this," Sam said. It was a large photograph in black and white of the man in the pictures with Aunt Grace. He wore the uniform of a naval pilot from the Vietnam era.

"Look at his face," Sam said.

I was already looking at it. That the face of the man in the photograph was the face of Sam's father I could well believe. The cheekbones. The high brow. The shape of the mouth. The clear deep-set eyes. The dark hair.

"Where did you find all this?"

She sat down on the arm of my wing chair looking down at the picture.

"After your father died," she said, "I found a chest with my mother's name on it in his closet. I found the key to it in the General's desk."

"What about those?" I nodded towards the sheaf of letters.

"They are love letters. Theirs. My father's and mother's. All except one."

She held up an envelope addressed in my father's handwriting.

"I don't think I want to read it," I said.

"Don't," she said. "Nobody really wants to become well informed on the subject of their parents' sex lives."

"No kidding."

"I've read them all. My father," she raised the black and white photograph, "was a pilot in Vietnam. He went missing in 1966."

"The year you were born."

"The year I was born. They met for the last time in Hawaii about a month before he … died, I guess." Her voice quavered.

"What was his name?"

"His name was Bill Rainer."

She looked at me questioningly.

"No," I said. "I never heard the name and I never saw the face. Except in yours."

"So you do see it," she said.

"I see it," I answered, "but I can't quite believe it."

To tell the truth, I wanted a drink and I wanted it more than I wanted to believe what I had begun to understand was true. That everything I'd done since I'd last seen Sam was somehow even more of a farce than I'd felt it was while I lived it. All my suffering was self-inflicted. But it wasn't unnecessary. I'd had to see just how low I could sink, and I hadn't hit the bottom yet. The thing I didn't know was whether Sam and I could build something like a life together after everything was sorted through. So I asked her.

"How long have you known all this?"

"I knew it all along in a way. I just didn't know I knew it."

"What does *that* mean?"

"I knew your father thought he was my father."

"How?"

"During the time he was dying, he said something that made me think that he was my dad … something about my mother."

"So you thought you were my sister when … the night …"

"No," she smiled. "I had already found the trunk and read the letters. Afterwards I came down and played the piano." She nodded towards it now.

"The Komodo Dragon Tree of Love," I said.

"Yes," she said. "The Komodo Dragon Tree of Love."

I closed my eyes and in just that instant was asleep.

22. Crossroads

I went to the crossroads

Fell down on my knees

Robert Johnson

I awoke towards dawn, shaking, sodden with sweat, oppressed by the fear that my world was tumbling down around me, though I had no clear sense of a world to which I belonged more than any other. It had been a rough night of strange dreams. Sam and I were alone adrift in a cold dark sea.

In the hearth, the fire crackled, scenting the room with cherry wood. An old crazy quilt was tucked around my feet. I could just hear Sam's voice from the kitchen. I thought she must be talking on the rotary phone that hung on the wall beside the kitchen table. When I tried to get up, my legs would not come under me. I sank back into the chair, exhausted by the little or nothing I had tried and failed to do. I watched the fire until sleep overtook me again.

I was startled awake by ringing, a bright shaft of light warming my face. My nerves were raw. No phone had ever been that loud anywhere. When I grabbed the arms of the chair, this time I managed to stand. Why was I so feeble? I began to string together in some kind of sequence the events of the last two days. Since Thursday morning I had eaten nothing besides a piece of cheesecake, some peanuts, and a pack of nabs. Even so the prospect of food revolted me. All I wanted was something brown and cold and wet with a bite to it. The phone screamed on. I tried to take a step and thought better of that idea, as I listened to myself trying to curse. Even if I could get to the kitchen, whatever I might say to whomever would be better left unsaid. So I watched the fire until the ringing stopped.

The sun was well on its way to the meridian. Noises of the city morning filled my ears. A street sweeper cleaning up the salt and the ice from yesterday's storm, sounds of motors, horns, and brakes, a dog yelping forlornly. Lightheaded, I stumbled to the kitchen. A place had been set at the table. My eyes were drawn to a pale blue envelope with Jack on it beside the ham sandwich, the glass of water, the three oatmeal raisin cookies. The envelope ended up in my coat pocket. I sat down more addled than hungry. The minute my feet touched the floor, the phone began to ring again. Before answering it, I spoke aloud to see if I could recognize my voice. It had undergone a sea change. "Flip me a fish," I sounded like a barking seal.

"Telephone," I gargled.

"Who the hell is this?" said Charles D. Bledsoe.

"Who the hell is that?" my underwater voice replied.

"Jack Shock," he said like someone else might say piece of shit.

"Right," I croaked.

"What are you doing in Sam's house?" Uriah Heep that he was, I knew that Charley-Boy had the terms of the General's will, not to mention his fiancée's inheritance, committed to memory down to the last colon and codicil.

"Sam's house? I'm in Jack's house, staring at a ham sandwich I plan to eat at my own kitchen table." I was no longer gargling, thank God, just a croak now and then. To drive the point home, I picked up the thing itself and began slobbering on a corner of it about a quarter of an inch from the receiver with great smacking of the lips and gums.

"Where is Sam?" he demanded a tad hysterically.

"Bear is bam?" I slobbered.

"Sam!"

"Sab?" I swallowed.

"Goddammit, Shock."

"I'm sorry," I said in my best tweedy English professor's voice, "I don't allow profanity on my telephone, especially at mealtime. Cheerio."

I hung up.

Despite the sodden state of my attire, the palsy in my right hand, and the stiletto of migraine throbbing above my left ear, I felt quite uplifted by my phone chat with Sam's intended.

After a few more bites, civilly chewed this time, I lost my appetite. Feeling gritty and grubby, I shambled upstairs to my old room, the room where the General had passed. Between the closet and the chest of drawers I found a change for everything I had on except my coat and boots. Once upon a time a pint of Jim Beam had slept on its back between the mattress and the box springs, but some well intended soul, probably my ex half sister, had moved it. Goddammit.

I threw my sweat-soaked clothes into a corner and walked naked into the hall and at the end of it, the second story shower. For the first time in months, I caught a glimpse of myself in a full length mirror. I was not a sight for sore eyes. My teeth, first of all, though I did occasionally brush them, were badly stained. Cigarettes to the tune of three packs a day had done that. But the teeth themselves seemed to be all there. My skin, dark as an old saddle the last time I'd looked at it, had faded to pink and white. I was thin, mostly bones and gristle. The old scars — appendix, car wreck, another car wreck — were all where they were supposed to be. There was a lot more hair everywhere than I remembered. But I recognized myself — my world weary Rembrandt self — lurking behind the disguise.

Pretty soon hot water came running over me, a lot of it. I soaped up and felt the pulse and throb of a real shower. The last time I'd washed this well, I stood beneath a small waterfall in the branch beside the cabin, sluicing myself on one of those sixty-degree days you get a shot at even in February south of the Mason-Dixon. Today felt a lot better. The phone commenced to ring again. I let it.

After a good long while I got out and dried off. I caught a glimpse of myself, much pinker now as I opened the medicine cabinet. I passed over the oxycodone — not my thing — for the old man's Boker straight razor and strop. I hacked away at my hair and beard until I didn't look quite so much like Rasputin. The clumps I flushed would have made matching hair suits for Ken and Barbie.

I tottered back to my bedroom, sitting down dead center on it, like I was going to sleep. Here I was in my third day without a drink, the dry spell that started with my need to talk to Sam. All that virtue for nothing. I held up my right hand. The tremor had slackened but was not quite gone. Cuts and scratches everywhere, like I'd been tying knots in a blackberry bramble. The fingers were long and thin and ringless, like Robert Johnson's in the cigarette picture. I remembered the day when I'd pulled my wedding ring off one of those fingers and dropped it into a beggar's hat in Guat City. He smiled like he'd won the lottery, poor fellow.

I decided to try my simian fingers on the old Gibson in the closet. The General had won it in a poker game in WWII. Someone, probably not me, had loosened the tension on the strings. I tuned the A string to pitch and the rest of them to that. What a voice that old Gibson had! I bent the E^7 notes, like a train whistle, on the first and second strings at the seventh and eighth frets, the same lick Scrapper Blackwell used in "Alabama Women" in 1934. Then I fingered the descending tremolo triplet E^7 chord from Willie McTell's "Feel Like a Broke Down Engine." Even though the rusty strings cut my fingertips like penknives, I kept on listening to my even rustier voice:

> *Feel like a broke-down engine*
> *Ain't got no driving wheel*
> *Ever been low down or lonesome?*
> *You know exactly how a good man feel.*

I kept on, forming the chords that Big Bill had used in the turnaround to "Key to the Highway" — E major to C sharp 7 to F flat to B^7 back to E, singing:

127

Trouble in mind,
I'm blue.
But I won't be blue always.
The sun's going to shine
On my back door someday.

My voice, roughened by bourbon and tobacco like the ridges on an old mill file, sounded like it meant what it sang.

After my fingertips got good and sore, I leaned the guitar against the chest of drawers and looked it over. It was dark brown like an old fiddle with a small burst, no bigger than my hand between the sound hole and the bridge. All in all, it made me think of me. Scuffed, dinged, cowboy chord divots on the fretboard, but still able to make music. It had one of those boat keel necks you find on guitars from the thirties. This axe, my old Duolian, and the cabin were the only actual things I'd missed while I was on my so-called sabbatical.

All the time I'd been playing, I kept thinking about Sam and about how much I wanted a drink. Sometimes the one made me think of the other. I'd sobered up to come home to bare the truth to the only human being I loved, but it was she who had bared it to me. Not a Keats or Rembrandt truth, a just-the-facts-ma'am truth. It would seem that that truth should have set me free, like Tom Jones with Sophie, to live happily ever after. But having the gates to Xanadu thrown open did not have the effect of freeing me from my reservations, not about her, but about myself. Far from it.

Maybe you remember the scene when Huck Finn has to decide between "hell" — Jim — or "heaven" — the Widow Douglas. Or to put it another way, between giving his best friend his life back or treating that friend as property and restoring him to the widow, Huck's own private jailer and killjoy. Easy call.

Or in *Tom Jones,* marry the beautiful Sophie and live happily and wealthily ever after. Easy call.

Lay the bottle down and marry Sam. Easy call. I'd have my life back with my own true love to share it with. But my impulse was still "Hide and if they find you, lie."

I freely admit that for a good long time now life as Jack Shock had been no great shakes. Self pity aside, if my life was a sorry one — and it was — I had nobody to blame but myself. Calling a spade a spade, a weak character and a strong thirst had bent my moral backbone into an oxbow. More than that, I'd come to like the brackish joys of the night life. I was no longer there to duck the botched marriage and the post modern blues. I wanted my bottled oblivion and here and there the ephemerality of the fleshly encounter, decked out as an affair of the heart. Brinksmanship. Or as the wizards of the Science Palace might say, an adrenaline rush. Jack Shock, staggering on a tightrope, over the abyss with "There she blows" on his lips.

If I was trying to kid anybody that brinksmanship was the same thing as love, the joke was on me. For all my contempt, not for Derrida, Foucault, and Lacan, so much as for what academia had made of them, they weren't mere drunks. At least they were trying to articulate, to put it euphemistically, a philosophy of our times. Lermontov had understood all that long ago. The jumble of drunkenness and sex my life had become revealed to me for what I was: a hero of our times in the best post-modern way. A cynical, incompetent dupe of his own attempt to escape the world of trouble and sin by taking the train to Blottosville.

If I wanted to drink until my liver gave out, I had that right. But I didn't have the right to make Sam watch it. Maybe I didn't deserve her. The kindest thing I could say about me was that I was a drunk who loved her. Unless some Jovian thunderbolt bounced me out of my barstool with my brain rewired, all I had to offer Sam beyond the grace of an early death was Dostoevskian melodrama.

I had had my fill for good and all of cheating and chain jerking and half love and south of the border surfer girls and bar bimbos and women who throw you out of cars on mountaintops. But I still had a powerful thirst. Many and many a time I had drunk from the bitter cup. Before I made any promise to Sam or anyone, I had to see if I could put some time together without Jim Beam *et al* as boon companions.

Time is all anyone has, come down to it. If I waited for Sam to come home, I'd say the right words all right, say love and mean it. But the right words don't make you act right. However much I wanted to, I didn't know if I had it in me to act right. It's not that I was chickening out before the hand was even dealt, but based on a solid track record of fuck-ups of many years standing, I had no faith that I could change. Most of all I didn't want a reprise of the night with Sam after the General's letter when I'd started the bender that, as far as I knew, was still on.

Speaking of letters, I had yet to read Sam's. I placed my fingertips on the edge of the envelope in my coat. In a trice I was reading its contents.

Dear Jack,

      I can't imagine my life without you being a part of it. I know you love me. I know you know I love you. Please don't leave. Wait for me.

      Love,

      Sam

      P.S. Charley may call. You know he is not your biggest fan.

      As I read this over, there was something missing from it that needed to be said. First, Sam had never mentioned that in less than a month she was going to marry Charley-Boy. Second, she seemed to have overlooked the fact that I was pretty much a basket case.

      In the chest of drawers, I found a white legal tablet. Collecting my thoughts as best I could, I said what had to be said.

Dear Sam,

      If you look into your heart, you'll see that what you feel for me is a tenderness for an old friend and a desire to save him — me — from himself. A life with me as I am now would degrade you, Sam, and I'm not sure that I can be saved or want to be. Even if you and I were lovers in your favorite Jane Austen novel, I would bet against me.

      I won't tell you to marry Charley. I don't care much for him though he's a better bet than I am. Please believe, there are many better men than either of us.

      If ever I can get my life back, if ever I can give my liver a reprieve, if one day I can stand to look at myself in the metaphysical mirror without ducking, I will come back to you, if only as a friend who loves you more than he loves himself.

      Jack

      I got up from the bed, still tottering some until I got a purchase, folded the letter and put it under Sam's door. I put my wet clothes in a paper sack and the Gibson in its case and walked downstairs with them.

      I stood in the kitchen for a final look around. I was the last of five who had once eaten as a family here — father, mother, sister, brother, all gone. I didn't know when or if I would see this place again, and none to tell me whether tonight I would be this close to sober evermore.

I tucked my shirt in my jeans and with the guitar in one hand and my sack full of wet clothes in the other walked out and back-latched the big red door. I never stumbled walking towards the Lincoln, wondering not for the first time if it would take me as far as Guatemala.

23. The Last Fair Deal

It was just before my wedding to his daughter that Jackson Prileau and his right hand man began to occupy a place in my imagination like none other.

Years before I met her daughter, Donna's mother, a socialite from Fairhope with a taste for the wild side, had absconded with a real estate agent. It bothered me that Donna never seemed worried by the fact that neither of them were ever heard from again. Not to sound melodramatic, but I'm morally certain that if I had gotten to know her father before Donna and I had our little moment in the rose garden off the West Range, I'd have enlisted in the Foreign Legion before I proposed to her. Daddy Prileau was the nearest thing to a psychopath I had ever met.

Of course, I blundered into him now and again during that last year at school when Donna and I more or less lived together. I noticed his stare when she smushed her body against mine. But how could I blame that. It's a rare father who smiles as his daughter throws herself at a young man who is flagrantly her sex pal. Only when I went down to Mobile did I get a full dose of Jackson.

The Prileau mansion made the White House look like humble pie. It was as big as a Wal Mart and a monument to pretentious bad taste. For appearances sake I had my own room in it of course: four-poster bed complete with pineapple finials, Chippendale desk. You get the picture. Every night Donna made her way to my room to ensure I got a thorough workout in that bed. The day before the wedding, I was trying to sleep off a hard night of road work when Jackson literally burst in with Colt .22 magnum revolvers in each hand. I seriously believed that he was about to shoot me.

"Get up, Jack," he said, "I need you." Grateful for at least a few more minutes of life, I got up and began to dress. I couldn't help noticing that the whole time he kept staring at my mid-section until I got my pants on.

Outside, a couple of picturesquely uniformed gardeners toiled on the lawn. In front of the house on the white pebbled semicircular driveway was Jackson's truck, a full sized extended cab with a tandem rear end. It was the only work truck I've ever seen with rolled and pleated white leather seats. Behind the wheel was a man whom I had glimpsed before only at a distance.

Although I couldn't judge just how big he was, I inferred from the coil of muscle in his biceps that he was a force to be reckoned with. His nose had been broken at least twice, so that it spread down his face in two distinct steps. On that nose was a pair of Cool Hand Luke prison guard mirror aviator glasses. Jackson did not bother to introduce us, and I was not eager to look this man in the eye, even supposing I could have seen his eyes. Jackson rode shotgun. I took a seat in the back directly behind the driver. The two Colts lay tip to tip beside me. Three tooled leather cases sheathing long guns leaned on the seat next to me.

Gradually, as I sat staring at his red scarred neck, I became aware of yelping behind me. Craning my neck, I saw a slat box about the size of a microwave. Donna's white pekepoo pushed his paw imploringly towards me, looking up at me and whining pathetically. What the hell, I thought. But I said nothing.

It was June, the season of weddings. The fields along the road were filled with knee-high corn. Jackson turned suddenly to smile at me. With his grey eyes, full lips and dark curling hair, he looked a lot like me. Or I like him. It was as if I could see myself years hence, as a soulless, heartless shell. Suddenly the truck stopped.

"Get out," he said. I got out.

"Get those shotguns, Sonnybuck." This was the first time I'd heard Jackson's Igor named. The name seemed comical given his brutal face. I tried not to stare at him, but I had never been that close to anyone that big and that ugly.

Then Jackson spoke to me.

"Jack. Get out and get that crate out of the truck bed."

A scenario was beginning to take shape in my mind that I didn't care to imagine.

"Why?" I asked, more sharply than I'd intended.

"Because that's a vicious dog," he said.

"Then take him to the pound."

"He bit the girl you're going to marry tomorrow."

"Well I didn't see any marks on her," I said.

He looked me up and down with a disgusted look, shaking his head.

"I want to see what you're made of before I let you marry my daughter," he said.

"I don't follow your train of thought," I replied.

133

Jackson laughed. That laugh, insulting and mirthless, hung in the air like a thunderhead, a prelude to violence. Jackson looked at Sonnybuck with his thumb cocked towards me.

"The professor here," — since Donna had told him that I'd been accepted into the graduate program at Chapel Hill, Jackson had taken to referring to me as the professor — "he can't follow my train of thought." Jackson pronounced the last three words as if they were an obscenity.

"What you think of that, Sonnybuck?"

For an answer the driver looked me in the face, hawked and spat. Jackson selected one of the long guns and removed from its case, an over and under Browning 20 gauge. He loaded it. At the same time Sonnybuck jerked the box to the tailgate, opened it and dragged from it a small shivering shrieking dog. The pekepoo bit his thumb and Sonnybuck took it by the ears and jostled it, coming close to breaking its neck.

"Get you one of those pistols, Jack," Jackson said.

"Is this a joke?" I knew it wasn't. For an answer, Jackson shouldered and cocked the shotgun and nodded at the driver. Sonnybuck swung the small white yelping bundle behind him like a bowling ball. As he released it, it sailed upwards and across Jackson's line of fire. Both barrels of the gun exploded at once.

"I got just one thing to say to you, Jack." He turned from the carnage he had made to face me.

"You fuck up, you gonna disappear."

******

It was just coming dark when I rolled into Charlottesville. Turning down Park Street, I hoped I might catch Rucker in his office before he drove home to Farmington, the city's snottiest suburb. I parked the Lincoln behind his Mercedes and let myself in by the back door.

Mounting the bull-nosed Victorian stairway, I saw Rucker's well fed form outlined in his office door. He certainly did look prosperous with his razor haircut, the second chin, a fawn colored suit of Harris tweed, and the tan cashmere topcoat draped over his arm, quite a contrast to his look back in the day: thin in tie-dyes and dreds, nailing down the backbeat for the Terraplanes on a pearl grey set of Ludwigs. He was my oldest friend in Charlottesville, yet I hadn't seen him once since I'd gotten back from C.A. I interpreted his silent head-to-toe inspection of my face and form as expressing potent disapproval. His law degree from the University had conferred upon him membership in country clubs where blacks were welcome only as servants and Jews weren't welcome at all. He had come a long way since his last gig with the Terraplanes, but I had liked him better skinny with dreds.

"Jack," he said, his voice as dry as a desert wind, "we meet at last."

"Rucker," I nodded. I decided not to attempt a hand shake. The tremors were worse now that I had no steering wheel to hold onto.

"Let's cut to the chase," I said with false bravado. "What's up with Donna?"

"She won't sign," he said, shrugging.

"Why the hell not?" I was so exasperated I almost snorted.

"Maybe the girl still loves you."

"Rucker. Donna's love is the Nile at flood, a mile wide and an inch deep."

"I've got worse news," he waited, fixing me with his eyes and nodding.

"Jackson Prileau is in town." Witnessing my expression, he laughed that dry professional laugh that he'd probably bill me for first thing in the morning.

I stood there for a moment, my hands in my pockets to hide the shakes, wondering why McFate had decided to gift me with Daddy Prileau, the only person in the world I'd less rather see than his daughter.

"He's out there right now," Rucker continued, jerking his head in the direction of the downtown mall.

"Where exactly is there?" I was looking down, shaking my head.

"I saw him in Fellini's. Your home away from home." Rucker gave me a good basting with one of those "you-fuck-up-you" looks that he seemed to make liberal use of since fortune had smiled on him.

"You're sure it was him?"

"Oh yes. Donna was with him. So was that quote chauffeur unquote of his. Built like Arnold Schwarzenegger. Talks like Slim Pickens."

"Sonnybuck." Uh-oh, I thought. Not good.

"That's the one," Rucker said, taking unseemly pleasure in his role as the bearer of evil tidings.

I smiled. "Maybe he brought Sonnybuck along to keep his daughter off Dice Street."

"Lame old Jack," he said. For a second as he caught my eye, his expression was almost human. Then he remembered our professional connection.

"How bad and how quick do you want to get shed of her?"

"I don't want her dead," I answered, deliberately misunderstanding his tone. "I just want a divorce."

"How soon?"

"Yesterday would be too late."

"I hear you."

"Do what has to be done."

"I have been. We can do this without Donna's signature. I've sent you documents to sign. Registered letters. It's like you don't even read your mail."

"I don't." I took out a cigarette and tamped it on each end on my watch face.

"What's that all about? Who doesn't read his own mail?"

I shrugged my shoulders and lit up. "I'm a drunk," I said. "I don't have time for it."

"You're not drunk now."

"I will be," I said. I wasn't just being rhetorical. I blew smoke rings to punctuate that fact. And then Sam's face flashed before me.

"So how in hell do I get you to sign what's got to be signed?"

"Hey, I'm here now. Take me up there and I'll sign away."

"And I'm on my way home. Look, Jack, I couldn't find that paperwork on a bet. Phyllis is the only person in this office who knows where that petition is."

I nodded. "I believe you."

"I'm on my way home, Jack. It's been a long day. Come in on a weekday when Phyllis is here — "

"Monday," I broke in.

"Monday."

I put my hand out, hoping he wouldn't notice it shaking. He stepped down, looking me in the eye and gave me the Dale Carnegie handshake.

"You look like hell, Jack."

"You look like … a lawyer, Rucker."

"You're a waste of skin," he said, his eyes smiling.

"You're another."

A joke from the days when we were roommates. One of Rucker's conquests had summed him up with just that phrase as she walked out the door one morning barefoot in a calico sundress with her bra slung over her shoulder.

136

We went out together with a little of the-way-it-used-to-be between us, not friends exactly, but as lawyer and client united in our mission to cut me loose from the poor little rich girl whom we both had known in the Biblical sense in her Junior League heartbreaker days but whom I had been stupid enough to marry.

"Good to see you, Jack."

"Just all right to see you, Rucker."

He laughed, shaking his head, "You going to let me out, Jack?" He pointed to the Lincoln.

I walked over to it, started up the Continental, and let him by.

*****

The first person I saw when I pushed through Fellini's front door was Eden. She was sitting on Jack Shock's own barstool in a tight black dress. When I walked in, she smiled at me like she'd been waiting all her life for this moment to arrive. I tried but I couldn't manage a smile back. Standing a little behind her on his side of the bar, Plunkett nodded at me and winked, pointing slyly at Eden. The girl herself stepped forward and gave me a kiss that was far from chaste.

"Tell me something, Eden."

She smiled at me and nodded.

"You're not a student, are you?"

"Of life ..." She was a playful tyke.

"How old are you?"

"How old do you want me to be?"

"Twenty-one. At least."

"I've been that."

"Good."

Plunkett had already extracted the Jack Shock fifth of Jim Beam from the freezer. Holding it out to me, he asked me with his eyes if I wanted the usual.

I thought of Sam. I shook my head. "Give me a black-and-tan," I said. These were words Plunkie had never before heard from Jack's mouth. He looked at me to see if he'd heard me right. I nodded.

"You've got it, Big Guy," he said.

Plunkett went down to the taps at the far end of the bar and signaled for me to join him. I gave Eden's shoulders a squeeze and left her to fend off the barracudas who closed in after Jack walked away.

Plunkett was leaning over the bar with a conspiratorial look.

"Where were you last night?"

"D.C."

"Anything wrong?" Lying, I shook my head no.

"The whole goddamn town came in here last night looking for you."

"The whole damn town?" He was nodding yes.

"At six, Susan comes in with that guy that looks like a junkie."

"Drew."

"Yeah. Drew. And she's almost crying. 'Where's Jack?' she says. And I say 'Not here.' She goes out blubbering with Drew bird-dogging her. Then in comes that lawyer of yours."

"Rucker Breeden."

"Yeah. That's the guy." And *he's* looking for you too. While we're talking, in walks Donna, her dad — a mean looking son of a bitch — and then an even meaner looking son of a bitch in a cowboy hat."

"His name is Sonnybuck."

"Huh?"

"My soon-to-be-ex-wife's daddy's hired assassin. Except I think it says 'chauffeur' on his W-2."

"Huh?"

"Never mind." I had just put my lips on the edge of the black-and-tan's mug. I put it down barely tasting it. I was looking over at Eden. She was flirting with one of the Fellini's barracudas.

"Then they leave, and an hour later Donna comes back in with an envelope. She writes your name on it, gives me a twenty, and asks me to give you the envelope when you come back in."

"Wow," I said. "Do I have to read it in your presence?"

Plunkett gave me a startled look. "No!" Then he nodded up the bar towards Eden. "A half hour ago *that* one comes in and sits on your stool. Look, Big Guy, don't you think she's a little ..."

"Young," I cut in.

"Wild," he said. "That girl — that girl — that girl is wiilldd!!! And she's a certified carpet muncher."

"I'm just her chaperone," I said. "But she's old enough to get into all the trouble she wants to."

"Gotcha," said Plunkett. He turned to a bottle of I.W. Harper on the shelf and took Donna's note out from under it.

"Here it is," he said. "Jack. You've got too many women in your life."

The more you got the less you have, I thought.

"Just one, really, Plunkie. Hope you meet her some day."

"Susan's a friend," he said. "Be nice to her." I nodded.

"What about Donna?"

"You're on your own there," he answered.

I walked over to Eden. Flirt that she was, she leaned her back past the barracuda with the grey pompadour and wolfish smile and cushioned herself against my chest.

"So what are we doing tonight?" she said smiling up at me.

"Do you dance?"

"I *love* dancing."

It had come to me on the drive over that there was one place that Daddy Prileau, Sonnybuck, and Donna would never set foot in. At least not together.

"Ever been to the Acid House?"

"Nuh-uh." Not much of one for talk was Eden.

As we were on our way out, Plunkett called out, "Hey, Jack, what about this black and tan?"

"Give it to Victor, but put it on my tab."

"No problem, Big Guy."

With that, Eden and I walked out onto High Street bound for the Acid House.

24. Hot Tamales and the Red Hots

Hot tamales and the red hots
Yes, we got 'em for sale.
Robert Johnson

Two fives got Eden and me hand stamps and admission to the Acid House in Live Arts, C'ville's version of the Blackfriars Theatre. Live Arts used the Acid House to cash in on the world beat phenom. The décor was flat black walls with a splatter of purple haze lit by track lights and strobes. The Acid House had become the showcase of the Kool. But I was there because of a redneck Nazi father-in-law.

It was just nine and already the place was packed, butt to butt and toe to toe. By the end of two minutes of Euro-tech, I was sweating freely. Keeping up with Eden I felt like I was dancing in leg braces. She had rubber bands for sinews. As she had said, the girl really did love to dance. She was fun to look at too: slinky with a great smile. I myself felt lucky just to be ambulatory. Still, I couldn't help smiling back at her every time I caught her eye. The more I danced the wetter I got, and oddly enough, the better I felt. The DTs had taken a sabbatical. I couldn't really get into the actual music. But the backbeat kept me at it. Humorless, sterile, implacable, and relentless, like a wood chipper with reverb.

Unlike the music Eden did have a sense of humor. She certainly didn't take anything seriously, especially me. To keep myself from bailing, I digressed into self-parody with a couple of pantomimes loosely describable as dancing: The Mouse — chiefly done with hands behind the ears — and the Potato Digger — a self-explanatory maneuver. What other woman in that room would have joined me in such lunacy? But Eden had the gift of a light heart. Or so I told myself. It was nice not actually knowing her story. Tonight, younger women, shorter stories was my anthem.

The L-shaped dance floor was about the size of a couple of basketball courts. As I glanced around I began to notice familiar faces. Reg the Surfer Boy, shed tonight of Vandillingham, had some bad moves going with a kindred spirit in the southwest corner. Both were arm wavers. In the same vein, there were a fair number of patrons of the Standard, two of whom ventured over to commiserate with Eden on her unfortunate pairing with me.

"You go girl," said the taller one.

"No, you come, girl," said his pear-shaped partner in a pseudo British accent, "dance with me."

Off they went leaving me potato digging and mousing alone as they shifted into Saturday Night Fever overdrive.

"Robbing the cradle again, Jack?"

I turned. Looking bemused and a tad miffed, Susan took me by the lapel.

"You're a better dancer than *that*." She had caught me in mid-Mouse, my thumbs behind my ears, palms outspread as I bobbed from side to side with a lobotomized smile.

"Maybe," I said. We had to shout to hear one another. "But give me Buckwheat Zydeco anytime over this stuff." I looked over her shoulder. "Where's Drew?" I wasn't actually missing him, but the Acid House was so obviously his kind of place that I couldn't imagine Susan here without him. Also Susan was dressed in Drew's hue, looking as she always did, startlingly vibrantly healthy and high colored, very un-Acid House.

Susan shrugged," I'm meeting him here — I guess ..."

"You look great," I said, "but black just isn't your color."

She had begun moving to the beat, her hand still on my lapel and it was easier to move with her than not to.

"Don't dance The Mouse when you're with me," she admonished.

"I promise."

"Or the potato thing."

"The Potato Digger," I corrected.

She was easy to dance with, but then I had memory to fall back on, for we had done our share of dancing in clubs back in the day when live music still ruled. Raising one hand, she got closer to me, never letting go of my coat, brushing against me with the parts of her I had never been able to forget. Three couples over Eden waved at me, still in thrall to the human pear, and I waved back.

"Looks like you're over Sam," Susan said.

"I'm not over anything."

"Have you heard from the department?"

"No."

"I heard they sent your case along to Dean Webley."

I started to ask her where she'd heard that but just then the Deejay amped up the volume and set the strobes on bombs away. The whole noir-clad floor morphed into riot mode. The strobes struck couples and triples, freezing them for an instant before flitting on. I saw Drew in freeze frame on his way over, Eden too was moving towards us, though every couple of feet someone tried to jump her bones. Renata, a steely-eyed Standard waitress from Dusseldorf, her blond hair dyed and cut Cleopatra-short, gathered Eden into her arms and chew-kissed her. Whether their liplock signaled sexual orientation or whether it was just a random overflow of dramatic impulse, both girls were giving it their all and the strobe made sure we all got an eyeful. Then Drew joined them and began slurping in Renata's ear. Renata, basketball center tall even without her nine inch heels, broke off her kiss with Eden to chewkiss Drew.

Suddenly, the blare died and the strobes flickered out. In the darkness Susan stood tiptoe whispering in my ear, "Whatever Renata's got in the way of STDs you and I will have before morning."

"Wouldn't it be pretty to think so," answered Jack.

Susan was looking over my left shoulder, eyes wide as she pantomimed "Uh Oh." The music and lights exploded again. I turned to see Donna Gordon Prileau wading through the bobbing heads and waving arms, strobe lit and dressed to kill.

She was scanning the room in a grid search for her favorite moving target. Sweeping my hat off, I ducked. When I bobbed up, my cheek stopped at Eden's breast and she was looking where Susan's eyes and mine were fixed.

"Who is that woman?" she yelled. She smiled down at me indulgently. "She was at Fellini's last night looking for you."

"She's his wife," Susan shouted.

"Oh, you've got a wife?"

I nodded wearily. The Acid House had suddenly lost its charm for me. Looking up at Susan, I pointed at myself and made walking fingers towards the far exit. I turned to Eden mouthing "I'll be back." "I'll be here," she mouthed, pointing to the floor. I fought my way at a half crouch through the throng to the darkest of the three exits. It was guarded by a Goth Amazon whose facial piercings brought to mind a store card of miniature fishing lures. With a snide look she shoved the door open, spilling me hat in hand into the cool wet night. I sat down on the back step, looking out on an alley with a view. High Street looked like it had been slathered with a coat of spar varnish. I put my hat on and automatically reached for a cigarette, finding instead the letter Donna had bribed Plunkett to put into my hands. I took it out and opened it, holding it aslant to catch the light of a street lamp. Though it bore neither signature nor salutation, it was Donna to the core: heavy cream-colored stationery, violet ink, hint of Chanel.

About time you read this. You're in a world of trouble, Jack. Remember those beach lots in Gulf Shores? The ones Daddy put in my name the year we married? Back when I used to think you hung the moon I put them in your name too. Daddy needs to sell them now. I mean NOW. I've signed. I advise you to do the same. He doesn't have any leftover sentimental feelings for you the way I do. Sonnybuck even less so. I'm warning you. Don't do something stupid.

I took her warning seriously enough to walk round the building to the main entrance to see if Sonnybuck and Pops were haunting its vicinity. If they were, I didn't see them. I walked back to the alley and sat down again, smoking. I got to thinking over the enigmas of Donna's behavior before and since I'd gotten back from Guatemala. Stalling the divorce, her various efforts were meant to throw me off balance. As if anyone needed to as I staggered towards catastrophe and suicide by Jim Beam.

I decided that it all boiled down to the God Almighty Buck. Real estate deeds in my name, some kind of tax dodge probably. I had no grasp of the niceties of the law: wills, deeds of trust, quitclaims, bills of divorce. But I was pretty sure that Donna and her daddy had grounds to fear that I'd have some claim to that beachfront property, closer to well-heeled Fairhope than to Mobile, if memory served. I reckoned that Donna and Daddy had kept us married just to ensure that ownership would pass to her if my ship went down. It did go down off Grenada, but too bad for them, without Captain Jack.

As always Donna had played me. When the grieving, love-struck spouse act didn't work, she'd teamed up with Bernie. Her testimony at my show trial was meant to bring me squarely under her thumb and to remind me of my mashability. No doubt there was the added joy of seeing me accused of what she had done to me. Yes, she had washed my face in my powerlessness. She had fought to level me beyond rehabilitation. Now I was getting my just desserts. She had warned me, for Christ's sake. Somewhere her daddy and Sonnybuck were plotting to impose on me the punishment that even pekepoos must suffer for biting the hand of Donna Gordon Prileau. I said her name aloud. The door behind me opened. A shaft of light illuminated a slender shadow, throttled by the door's closing. My incantation stood before me, smiling at the spectacle of her nemesis with her letter in his hand.

I addressed her in the old hectoring style: "Donna, my love, what do I have to do to get your old man and his scrapple-faced Igor out of my life forever?"

She took a drag off her Virginia Slim and smiled, wreathed in an aura of tobacco smoke.

"You could die," she said.

"Don't want to," I answered.

"You could sign off on those beach lots." She took another drag.

"Ah …"

"You look like hell," she cut in.

"Yeah," I said, "I've noticed."

"Really. I mean it."

She was looking me over like she used to look over her bay gelding, the one she rode to hounds on with Farmington, just before she slipped the wire snaffle with the curb chain in his mouth.

"Yeah," I said again, "I'm looking scruffy these days."

She looked me over more carefully and drew back, startled.

"I know what it is. You're not drunk."

"No," I admitted. "For once."

"Why?"

It was a good question, one that still didn't have an answer. Normally, I'd have continued to assail her here in the old style, calling her "Lambie Pie" just to keep the strife at high tide. But instead I stood up.

"I need a change."

"Amen to that," she said.

We smoked a while standing there, glancing at each other once in a while as if we were familiar strangers. And on my part there was something like regret for all the time we'd spent making each other miserable to no purpose at all. Donna took a long last drag on her cigarette.

"I'm sorry I lied at the trial thing."

"You didn't do me any harm," I said. "I could give a fuck about my professional life."

"I was so angry with you, Jack."

"Yeah. Join the club."

"You're so damn passive-aggressive."

"Guilty," I said raising my right hand.

"Sometimes I just want to see you break down and beg."

"Yeah," I said. "That game ain't worth the candle."

"No," she said. "I ain't." She was still holding the cigarette, burned right down to the filter. She tossed it.

"Sign the release, Jack."

"Sure," I said." "Why not?"

She shook her head. "I don't believe you."

I shrugged.

"Don't go to war with my daddy."

She was looking at me earnestly, which is a word I didn't ever remember thinking in connection with Donna before.

"He doesn't like you."

"Don't I know it."

"He'll hurt you if he can."

"Why did you get him up here, if you didn't want me hurt?"

"It was his idea."

I raised my eyebrows.

"It was." She lit a cigarette and sat down on the step. She was looking up at me.

"Don't go home," she said.

"Why not?"

"He went to the cabin last night."

I sat down beside her.

"He did?" The idea of him waiting for me out there in the mountains in the one place I felt safe from whatever wolf was at the door took the heart out of me.

"Was Sonnybuck with him?"

She nodded.

"They spent the night."

"Not much to do out there. No dogs to shoot."

She shook her head in disbelief.

"Don't you care?" she asked. "He's got a gun."

"Your father?"

"They both do."

I winced.

"They said you live like a damn monk."

"Yeah. A drunk monk with a three-pack-a-day Camel Jones."

"You can't go back there, not tonight."

"I agree."

"Can't you stay with someone?" I said nothing. "What about Susan?"

"What about her?"

"Can you stay with her tonight?"

"Don't think so," I said. The least I owed Susan, or anyone, with the possible exception of Vandillingham, was to keep her out of Sonnybuck's line of fire.

"What about the blonde?"

"You're the blonde."

"Young. Looks like Barbie. Easy."

Takes one to know one, I thought. "Her name is Eden," I said.

Donna raised her eyebrows.

"Are you fucking her?"

"Maybe," I said.

"Can you go home with her?"

"Maybe."

"Do it," she said. "Don't go home tonight. Don't go back to Fellini's. Don't go to your car."

"OK," I said without conviction.

She shook her head.

"You don't have a gun, Daddy said."

"No," I answered. And suddenly I remembered that I hadn't told the truth. But I said again, "No."

"I've got to go, Jack."

"Go."

"I told Daddy I'd look for you."

"I figured."

"I'm not going to tell him I found you."

I wondered about that for a moment but she seemed to be in some distress and I reckoned she was probably telling the truth.

"Uh-huh" was all I said.

"Maybe I can set up a meeting for tomorrow."

"High Noon outside the police station would be nice."

She looked at me smiling sardonically.

"I don't think Daddy will go for that but I'll try." She was lighting another cigarette.

"How do I get hold of you?"

"Leave a message with Rucker."

She thought about that.

"I don't think Daddy will meet you at Rucker's either."

"Rucker won't sully his hands with my problems with your father. He'd probably refuse to let Sonnybuck on the premises."

"Probably," she said. "Rucker was always short in the nerve department."

"I don't know that nerve is my long suit either."

"You don't give a damn," she said. "You've got that kind of nerve. It could get you killed."

"Didn't you just tell me I could die?"

"I don't want you dead," she said. Against all logic she threw her arms around me and hugged me just a second or two. "Damn you," she said. She stood up.

"I'm not going to tell Daddy I saw you." Then she said it again for the third time as if she had to convince herself. "Try to go home with a girl. Take her straight home and keep her occupied." She poked at me. "They found the Lincoln."

I guess she could tell I was trying to remember where I'd left it.

"Fellini's," she said poking my sternum. "Don't go there either."

"Right."

"Take care, Jack."

She'd begun walking. She looked good on the move. She stopped and turned.

"I'll sign the papers and send them over to Rucker. The divorce," she said.

"OK. Thanks." I stood up and touched my temple and pointed at her by way of goodbye. I watched her walking down High Street past the wine shop, the parking garage, the police station.

I sat down again, thinking over my options. I owed it to Eden to keep her out of this, but I didn't want to just ditch her. So I knocked on the Acid House back door and the dour faced Goth Summo Wrestler finally let me in after pretending not to remember that I was one of the two people who had come through that door in the last ten minutes. I made my way over to Eden during a lull in the din. She was dancing with Renata. Limey was drooling over

Reg. I didn't see Drew or Susan but I didn't really perform a searching and fearless inventory either.

"Hello, Beautiful," I said.

"Jack!" She threw her arms around me.

"I thought you might be going home with your wife."

"We haven't been surfing together in quite some time."

"Surfing," she smiled. "Is that what you call it?"

"Depends on what you mean by 'it.'"

"It is It," she said.

"You've got that right," I said. "How long will you be here? Till it closes?"

"At least," she said.

"Then what?"

"There's an after-hours party at the Standard."

"Sounds good."

"Will you come?"

"I will."

If I live, I thought. And kissed her goodbye on the cheek.

25. Midnight Hour Blues

In the wee midnight hours
Long about the break of day
When the blues creep up on you
And carry your mind away.

Leroy Carr

As I opened the main exit door at the Acid House, I saw Sonnybuck step out of the shadows, looking for someone or something. As unobtrusively as I could, I fell back around the corner and hunkered down against the rain-slick walls.

I half expected to see Sonnybuck or Daddy Prileau rush me, but Donna was true to her word. After a while I began making my way up High Street. A hundred yards or so along, I crossed the street at a dead run and disappeared into an alley just this side of the county office building where I squatted on my heels to catch my breath. Then I turned down Main Street, hugging the store fronts heading down the mall towards Whitey's.

In the eighties Main Street had been closed off to traffic and paved over with new old-looking red brick. Here and there among the potted trees you glimpsed flat black steel silhouettes of larger-than-life representatives of the Rotarian clientele the city council hoped would flock downtown instead of people like me and the two thugs on my trail.

At a cross street roughly opposite the entrance to the Acid House, I pulled up short and, hat off, peered around the corner. Before me a group of men were standing and smoking and talking. From a distance they were a rough looking bunch, but as I moved towards them, their tattoos and biker garb were less noticeable than a genial if gnarly solidarity. One of them, tattooless, in a hat I might have worn, called out my name, startling the hell out of me.

"Hey, Jack. Jack Shock, I guess I should say Professor Shock. Don't you know me?" He swept off the hat so I could see his face.

"I took Modern American Literature from you in McGregor Hall in the eighties. Aced it. Probably the only guy who did. You were pretty stingy with A's."

I did know his face now but not his name; it was on the tip of my tongue.

"Hello, brother," said a behemoth beside him with a shaved head. I shook his hand.

I turned back to my former student and shook hands with him too. I remembered his frequent interpolations in class in a cool commanding voice always with a half-masted wave of his arm. He showed a post modern irreverence for anything he hadn't given his permission to exist, but compared to the professionals of McGregor Hall he was strictly bush league.

"You're Angleton, right?" I asked, "First name, Kai."

He put his hand out again; I shook it for the second time. I noticed that he was wearing a jacket something like the one I had on but even more holed and frayed.

"Do you work here?"

"No," he said. "I'm not one of the professionals, just another inebriate."

"He means alcoholic," said the behemoth winking at Kai.

Kai was thinner and taller than I remembered. For a long time his beard and his hair had known neither comb nor scissors. His clothes fit him as if he had randomly picked them off the rack at the Goodwill or the Salvation Army.

Faraway, with something like an inner gasp, I glimpsed a familiar shape, or rather two of them: Sonnybuck and Daddy Prileau were standing on the steps of the Acid House scouring the spillover from the dance floor, collected in couples, triples, grouplets, many smoking here and there, some taking a hit off a bottle. From their body language I knew Daddy and Sonny hadn't found who they were looking for. I felt a sudden self-serving urge to join the communion of the tee-totaling bikerless bikers.

"Is there some kind of meeting in there?" I gestured toward the doorway over which was written "The Haven" in stenciled letters.

"A meeting of the Living Sober Brotherhood is about to start," announced a short balding man in wire-rim Coke bottle glasses and a leather vest.

"Come on in, Jack," said Kai.

"You might hear something in there that will change your life," said Coke bottles.

Sonnybuck's eyes seemed to be straining towards Kai in the group I was a part of. I went in with the others without a backward glance. I found myself in a room about the size of my cabin. Everyone was talking, laughing, slapping the late comers on the back. No one slapped mine. On a table was a percolator filled with coffee, strong and black — Maxwell House by the smell of it. I took my Styrofoam cupful and sat down next to Kai, who had his hat on again as did I. Everybody seemed to get a kick out of the two of us. "Kai's got himself a sponsee," said the biggest guy in the room. I later heard him say his name was Steve.

Once the meeting had begun, the Sam tapes started playing in my head, so I missed a lot of what was said. I was given something to read and everyone read some of it. One phrase caught in my mind: "half measures availed as nothing." "Availed" is not a word you hear every day, especially not from the mouth of a biker with a shaved head and a tattooed teardrop on his cheek.

I didn't count them but there were probably twenty in the room, black, white, and brown, none of them women. Kai was running the meeting although that's not really how it felt. He talked a little about his life as a homeless street drunk. I gathered he hadn't been sober that long, months at most. He said he had to learn how to let go of his false pride to learn how to be right sized. I had never heard that phrase used to describe a human being before. The others looked at him, some of them nodding. When he was done, people raised their hands and he called on them. Some of the men were raw falling-down street drunks; one of them had the shakes so bad, he squeezed the arms of his chair until his fingers went white. I noticed that my own hands were as bloodless as his. Then *my* teeth started chattering too. I nodded at him and he nodded back at me with a hint of double take. Maybe he thought he knew me and, hell, maybe he did. I was too absent spirited to pursue that thought or any other.

When everything was over, we joined hands in a muddled circle and said the "Our Father" with "the power and the glory" ending. I was ready to bolt as soon as I turned loose of whoever's hands I held. I looked around me like a shoplifter who spots a store detective and strode quickly for the door. Kai was at my side; he put his hand on my shoulder as I caught at the door handle.

"Jack," he said. I turned without looking at him.

"Yeah." My eyes were on my boots.

"You said 'I'm Jack and I'm a drunk' when it came your turn."

"Yeah." I had the door open, hat in hand, peering out again at the Acid House.

"Back when I was a student, you were kind of my hero," he was saying. For the first time tonight, maybe even in my life, I looked him in the eye a little taken aback by his confidence.

"Why?" I asked, startled at being anyone's.

"My father was already dead. My mom died while I was at school. Hell, I liked the way you came to class looking like you had been on a bender the night before. I even started drinking in bars at night hoping maybe I'd run into you."

My eyes were on him, but I had nothing to say. What a role model I had made for an orphan.

"Look," he said, "I've got to clean up after the meeting. I'll hang out for an hour or so tonight in case you feel like coming back. I'd like to help you if I can. Maybe I could tell you my story."

"Thanks, Kai," I said. I had been avoiding him all these years as I had avoided all my students, except the exceptionally good looking women who came after me with extracurricular projects on their minds. Even those, I had never tried to know. Yet something in me wanted to stay and hear his story, but tonight my mind was preoccupied with the two men out there who according to Donna were not only willing to kill me but wanted to. I took a last look at this man who looked like a scarecrow version of me. Then I went out the door leaving him and his fellow travelers on the path to their chosen brand of salvation.

I saw no one either close in or far out, so I entered the mall heading south again. I began hearing a violin in the distance. A clock in the window of Tuel's Jewelers told me it was eight minutes to midnight, neither the time nor the season when you expect to hear "Somewhere Over the Rainbow" in the streets, played in the style of Pappa John Creech.

The fiddler had taken a stand across from some steel chairs sheltered from the rain by Whitey's awning. His dark fedora had its rippled brim turned down, his face under it splotchy and the nape of his neck dappled white with acne scars. His wire-rim glasses had thick eye-shrinker lenses. A violin case lined with green felt lay half open at his feet; in it were a few bills and some change. His melancholy expression suited the song and his playing of it. I opened my wallet and dropped a ten in. He bowed, glanced quickly at the bill and bowed again more deeply. He might have bowed a third time if he'd known his sole visible audience at that hour had just four dollars left in that wallet.

Outside under the awning at one of the steel mesh tables on either side of Whitey's entrance, I could see through the misted window that whoever was playing that night had gone on break. So I sat alone on a cold wet night listening to the busker fiddler playing Fats Waller's "I Can't Give You Anything But Love." I wasn't sure I had that to offer anyone anymore, but I liked the way he played the song. A clatter of heels sounded further up the mall. Soon I could make out Eden's white blonde head and a little bit later, her laugh. She was with Susan and Drew. Then she saw me.

"Jack, she called. "Is that you?" I didn't answer. By then I had seen who had stopped on a dime at the sound of my name fifty yards or so behind her. It was Sonnybuck.

As I watched him, Eden and Susan broke away from Drew and ran to me holding hands. Alcohol and the sardine can ambience of the Acid House seemed to have made them sisters for the moment. Each of them took me by a hand and tugged.

"Get up, Jack; there's a party at Eastern Standard," Eden trilled breathlessly.

"Not one with dancing," I replied, standing for a moment before gravity had its way with me and I slumped back. The Standard had little enough room for its ambulatory clientele, let alone for dancers.

"I hear *you* dance after hours on tables," Susan said, turning to face Eden.

"Naked as a jaybird, so they say," Eden said, looking at me.

"Well then," Susan replied also looking at me, "Jack will be there."

"I'll be along later," I said. I was watching a shadow in the doorway to Snooky's Pawn, a couple of hundred feet away. I didn't like to think about him anywhere near Susan or Eden.

"Drew," Susan called out, "we're going to Eastern Standard."

Drew joined us, talking as he walked. "Plunkett is going to drink five shots of Jaggermeister at 12:15 while he's on the phone to Mark and Roman."

I tried to visualize this feat, sure that beyond the glug-glug, there was no point to it. All three were bartenders known to pour the bar away at the drop of a hat. I knew I did not want to stay where I was and I did not want Sonnybuck following Susan and Eden. I didn't mind so much if he drew a bead on Drew, literally or figuratively.

"Come on, Drew," I said jumping up from the table. "It's almost 12:15." We left the girls laughing as he joined me at a dead run to Fellini's door.

As we walked in, Plunkett had the phone in one hand and a shot glass in the other brim-filled with what looked like burnt motor oil. "Hey, Jack! Come in. The Jaggermeister swigfest is about to begin."

"That's why we're here, Plunkie."

Plunkett already had an audience. Seated at the bar were a half-dozen provocatively dressed sorority sisters wearing Tri Delt pins and lop-sided leering smiles.

"Jack — Professor Shock," cried a brown-eyed red head with a body that Titian might have painted. I recognized her as a scholar manqué from way back who tended bar at the Biltmore, a student bar on the Corner a couple hundred yards from the Founder's Rotunda. She had been an entertaining though trifling member of one of those "Great Books I Happened to Have Read" seminars that lightweights like me taught in summer school.

Her rowdy sisters were egging her on with cat calls and howls.

"Well, hello, Catherine," I said. "I thought you'd graduated in '89."

"I am in my eighth and — possibly — final year, Jack."

Her pretense of dignity was undercut when she poked a finger through a tear in my jacket and traced a circle on my short ribs.

Buffy, Muffy, Puffy, Duffy and Tuffy shrieked with delight.

You don't come to see me anymore," said Catherine with mock sadness.

I considered the accusation. Yes, vaguely, I remembered an after-hours night at the Biltmore when a fleshly encounter loomed — before we drank ourselves out of the impulse.

"Catherine, I definitely would have come by if I'd only known you were on the eight-year plan."

Predictably, the Muffies dissolved again into a cacophony of howls, shrieks and sniggers.

"Tell him what we're doing," said one of them.

"We're drinking Sex On The Beach in every bar from here to the Biltmore," said Catherine, poking me again.

"We started at the C&O," said another Muffy.

"Wow!" I said. "Are you going to drink Sex On The Beach at the Black Elks Club too?" Plunkett pointed next door.

All six of them shook their heads and mouthed NO.

"Probably not a good idea," said Mick, who was pouring the last of their drinks. "I doubt the brothers would pour you a drink if you asked for Sex On The Beach."

The Muffies giggled.

"Are you driving," Plunkie asked, "or walking?"

"Staggering." This from a sloe-eyed brunette with a very pink face.

"Lurching," added a blonde with a Pepsi commercial smile.

"Crawling," said Plunkie.

They took up the word, chanting it in unison.

Just then I happened to glance out the window. Sonnybuck stood gazing in at the scene smiling, if you could call it that.

"Who *is* that guy?" asked Mick.

"A murderer from Mobile," I answered.

"I'm out of here," said Drew suddenly, who had been sulking in the corner, chewing his post modern cud. He swung the door open, giving Sonnybuck a wide berth.

Even with all of us looking at him now, Sonnybuck had eyes only for me.

A moment of clarity illuminated the fog of my mind. I decided forever that I was only too willing to sign whatever he or Daddy Prileau put before me. What the hell did I care about beachfront real estate on Alabama's Gulf Coast?

But Donna had said that matters had moved beyond the point where my signature would cause the two to disappear. I had fucked up and tonight on the Downtown Mall, like Donna's lap dog, I was destined to disappear. Minutes after Jack Shock hit the bricks, Sonnybuck and Daddy Prileau would be on the interstate bound for Mobile. My death was as good as my signature. Better.

Seeing all this I cannot explain why I stepped out from the safety of the crowd of benign hell raisers, who despite my wealth of shortcomings actually seemed to love my company. I opened the door and went out.

26. You May Bury My Body

You may bury my body
Down by the highway side
So my evil spirit can take a greyhound bus and ride.

Robert Johnson

"I got you, you son of a bitch," he said, grabbing me by the forearm. He looked like he could hardly believe his luck.

Staring into his face, I saw that the intervening years had done it no favors. It was pinkish red and cratered like some alien moon. The broken nose had been broken again. The middle of it was wide and flat like the nose on a porcelain doll. One of his eyes had a drooping lid, the eye beneath caramel-colored with bloodshot whites. The other one was mottled muddy-green with no whites at all. He was not smiling but his mouth was open, like a moray eel's as if it meant to bite. A canine was broken at the gum line, all his teeth as ill assorted and contradictory as if the set had been assembled from the leftovers of many mouths, not all of them human.

"Mr. Prileau wants to talk to you." He pronounced it *pray-loo* like it was two words.

"But I don't want to talk to him."

"You're coming."

"I don't think so."

Mick appeared behind me at Fellini's door.

"You all right, Jack?" He was looking at Sonnybuck's forearm. Very deliberately he moved from the doorway to Sonnybuck's blind side.

Then Plunkett came through the door with the Fellini's poker. Behind him was Catherine, a cigarette wedged in the corner of her mouth, her eyes narrowing with the smoke. The Muffies kept watch at the windows on either side of the door, highball glasses raised.

"You all right, Jack?" Mick asked again.

I looked at the poker resting like a scepter, point up on Plunkett's right shoulder. In moments like this one, the genie being out of the bottle, he favored reckless violence. But Sonnybuck's eyes never left my face.

"Who's the Mega Goober?" asked Catherine, blowing smoke into the mix.

A handful of the brothers who had been hovering around the entrance to the Black Elks Club flowed out, looping around me and behind Sonnybuck. For a moment I thought I saw Robert Johnson's shade among them.

"Who the big dude?" one whispered.

You would have thought that Sonnybuck's grip might have loosened a notch. The only thing that had moved was his free hand beneath his jacket along his belt to the spot where in former days he had kept a Colt 1911 semi-automatic.

That possibility decided me. I turned to face everyone except Sonnybuck.

"I'm going to take a short walk with Sonnybuck." I gestured backwards with the thumb of my free hand. "He's from Mobile and he does piecework for my ex-wife's father, Jackson Prileau."

"You ain't her ex yet," said Sonnybuck. "That's the problem."

"Right," I said. "I should be back in a half hour." I noted Catherine's concerned skepticism. "I'm all right," I said to her. "You can go back in. I'm all right."

I thanked all of them and then each in turn by name as they returned to the bar.

"Turn me loose," I said to Sonnybuck.

Sonnybuck turned loose of my forearm. I twisted it back and forth to get the blood flowing. He gestured towards the mall with his head.

Mick had stayed and was lighting a cigarette. "I was coming out for a smoke anyway," he said.

"Don't worry, Mick," I said.

"I'll be looking for you, Jack," he said. "You hear that, Mobile?"

Sonnybuck smiled that wonderful smile.

"Thanks, Mick," I said. "I'll be back."

Of all places, Jackson Prileau was waiting for me upstairs at Whitey's, the one bar where there was live music and a crowd. Skipper Brown had the bar; we exchanged telegraphed hellos. Sonnybuck and I walked along the bar, past the musician strumming an old Ovation guitar. It was a guy named Dave who had worked there two years ago when he had a Mr. T haircut." Eyes half-closed, he was singing "All Along the Watchtower," as if everything in his world depended on it.

Sonnybuck reached the stairs ahead of me and waited, nodding up with his eyes lifted. I mounted the stairs.

In one of the booths Daddy Prileau sat alone facing me. I sat down across from him, the one man in my life — far more so than dear old Bernie — who despised me more than I did myself, though for different reasons. He glanced at Sonnybuck, who went to stand guard at the head of the stairs.

"Well, well, well," he said. "Look what the cat done drug in."

"What can I do for you, Jackson?" said Jack Shock.

"Read this," he said gleefully, tossing me an envelope that had been sliced open from the top.

I did my usual Kabuki dance with the envelope, taking my time opening it up, fumbling for spectacles I didn't in fact own, but I did manage thereby to dampen his spirits. I read it through its contents and tossed it on the table.

"So?" I said.

"You've been canned."

"More or less," I replied. To tell the truth, I actually felt elated. Better yet, free.

"Don't you want to know how I came by it?"

I noticed my address and that of the courier service the University used for urgent business on the envelope. "At my cabin, right?"

I pulled my cigarettes from my shirt pocket and lit one.

"If you think losing a job I don't want is going to make me fall on my sword, Jackson, you are in for a letdown."

I blew smoke, not at him but above him, in three perfect rings and then coughed out the rest, spoiling the effect.

"This isn't your night, Jack," he sneered. "That letter is the least of your problems."

Actually, I thought the letter was a godsend. It said that I had been relieved of my teaching duties. Someone else would be taking on my two classes. I was to hand in all my course records. Cheers, Bernie! And good luck finding those course records. I would continue to receive my salary until Thorton Webley, Dean of the Faculty, in consultation with his administrative peers, determined my fate. Guatemala, here I come.

"Is that letter why you got me up here?"

For an answer, he brought up three legal looking binders and laid them down one by one like a hand of blackjack. He tapped on the first one with his index finger.

"Alabama," he said. "Read this one first." He placed a gold Mont Blanc pen on top of the binder.

158

I took my time getting hold of it. It was a quitclaim or some such mechanism embroidered with legal jargon by which I was to relinquish my ownership of the waterfront property. I signed it and slid it across to him, ending my brief tenure as a Gulf Coast real-estate magnate. He looked it over and nodded.

"You're lucky to be alive, Jack."

"We all are."

"You might be lucky a little while longer if you sign the others." He tapped on the middle portfolio.

"What if I don't want to be lucky? I'm getting bored with it."

He looked over my left shoulder toward the Sonnybuck shadows of the room.

"What do you think, Sonnybuck?"

"I love a chance to beat hell out of the sumbitch."

As Daddy Prileau sniggered with full throated ease, I joined in with my own Post Modern English Department version of canned laughter.

"Smartass," said Sonnybuck.

"Let me ask you something." I turned around to face him and then turned back to Jackson Prileau. "What are you two going to do if someone comes up here while you're killing me?"

"I rented this whole upstairs, Jack," said my father-in-law, "just to have you to myself."

"Thanks, Dad," I said. I was trying to egg him on.

"The only reason you are still able to run your mouth is that my daughter entertains some sentimental feelings for you."

His face actually beamed with self-satisfaction. Yes, Jackson Prileau finally had me where he wanted me. Where he had always wanted me. You could see it in his glistening eye, in the shine on his cheeks. He was in control now; this moment proved irrefutably that he had always been in control. I had thwarted his design yesterday by not being at the cabin. I could picture him and Sonnybuck taking their wrath out on the décor as they ransacked the house. Tonight, I had thwarted him again at the Acid House, but here I was at last, quaking in my boots. Except, I wasn't. And though he had me by the short hairs, he had fallen off considerably in my estimation from the nemesis of days gone by.

I noticed for the first time the broken blood vessels in his cheeks, the kind I had seen on the faces of lushes, street drunks, and rummies at the Living Sober Brotherhood. Hell, probably under the beard, I had some myself. His eyes too had lost the predatory gleam of yesteryear. Once that gleam had made me flinch but not tonight. Oh, he was still formidable. The square shoulders and bull neck — they were still there. And he was still a hateful, heartless son of a bitch. But right now I wasn't intimidated. I didn't care enough about my well being to be intimidated. I hated his guts and I had nothing left to lose.

"Sign," he said.

"What am I signing?"

He put his finger first on the binder I had signed and touched each in turn.

"Alabama. Virginia. Life."

I opened up Virginia and read through it quickly. I closed it without signing and without looking at him. I took up the third binder. It contained an insurance policy on my life for a million dollars. I closed the binder and looked at Daddy Bigbucks and laughed. "Dream on," I said. I heard Sonnybuck move behind me.

"If my blood falls on these documents …" I said.

Jackson Prileau raised his right hand at Sonnybuck and shook his head. I heard him step back. The smell of the cheap cologne that Sonnybuck preferred to bathing evanesced.

"Sign," he said.

I took up Virginia, the binder containing the deed to my cabin and land in Nelson County, opened it, and beside the X, wrote "Curly, Moe, and Larry," and slid it back to him. He opened it and read. His face grew grim.

"You're Curly," I said. "I'm Moe. He's Larry," pointing backwards with my thumb.

"Sonnybuck," he said, "come over here." He pointed at me. "Mash him," he said.

Before he got there, I lifted both my legs and kicked Daddy as hard as I could in both shins with my boot heels. I don't know where I got the courage to do that, but during the beating I took over the next few but very long minutes, I treasured what I had done. If I hadn't managed to get my arms between the table and my head, Sonnybuck would have killed me. For some post modern reason, my mind kept repeating a phrase I'd heard once in a department meeting, "The so-called Great Books are mere patriarchal sentimentalism."

It ended when I heard someone scream behind us on the stairs. As the slamming of my head on the table top ceased, a clamor of screams and shouts erupted. I was looking at my hat on the floor, and when I reached for it, I fell. I don't know how long I stayed there half conscious. Eventually, someone helped me up. It was Skipper Brown.

160

"Are you alright, Jack?"

"Been better," I tried to say.

"Who were those guys?"

"Fably," I said. Then I slipped into a brownout again.

Later, downstairs, after some commiseration and a plastic bag of ice for my left eye, I made my way back to Fellini's. The Sex on the Beach crowd were gone. Mick and Plunkett told me how attractive I looked with the blood caked in my hair, in my nose, in my beard, as I stood beside the urinal washing my face in the sink. I was just glad I still had my teeth. Both eyes were swollen, the left one more so. My nose was a mess. Sonnybuck had been very thorough in his efforts to recontour it along the lines of his own.

"So, Jack, why did they beat you up?" asked Plunkett.

"Money."

"Money? You don't have any money, do you?"

"I have great expectations."

"You're a pip, Jack," said Mick.

Charlottesville bartenders. All of them had college degrees. About half of them were English majors.

"What are you going to do?" asked Mick.

"I'm going over to the Standard to see Eden and Susan to tell them I'm leaving."

"Home?"

"Guatemala."

"You mean Guatefuckingmala," said Mick.

"What about your classes?" asked Plunkett.

"Easy come, easy go."

Mick had already signed out and he wanted to go with me. We had just reached the end of Second Street, when the shot rang out down the mall, reverberating off the brick and stone walls along it.

"Fucking A," said Mick. "Was that what I think it was?"

Something told me I didn't want to go up there. That I knew what I would find. But I blocked it out. I started walking towards the last echoes of the sound. Mick was beside me smoking.

"You think it's the Mega Goober?"

I nodded.

"Someone shot him?"

I shook my head no.

"*He* shot someone?"

I nodded.

"Who?"

Someone dressed like me, I thought. But I said nothing.

He was lying on his left side, his wide brimmed hat crushed under his face, his left arm under his body, his right one tucked close to his side with the palm upward, like an open claw. The eye that I could see was also open as if he had seen what was coming and was unappalled by it. Steve the biker was kneeling beside him crying silently, the tears glistening on his tattooed face. I felt my own eyes swimming.

"Did you see what happened?" I asked him.

"No," he said, "I was inside." The tears were sliding down his face so fast that they left long wet runnels.

Two men whom I had seen at the meeting arrived and knelt beside Kai. One of them put his arm around Steve.

"I was his sponsor" Steve was saying. "I was Kai's sponsor." He repeated that again and one more time and then fell silent.

"I know that guy," Mick whispered to me, looking down at Kai, "I can't tell you how many Vodka tonics I served him back in the day. I heard he quit."

I nodded. "He did quit."

"Why would anyone want to kill Kai?"

"They didn't," I said. I couldn't go on.

Mick shook his head. "The poor son of a bitch."

Up the mall, three policemen had someone cornered in the alcove of a store front. One of them carried a sawed off shotgun. I was hoping that my father-in-law or his protégé were in that alcove and would give him an excuse to use it. But a moment later a young black man emerged, walked, and then ran down the mall. After a while Mick and I turned and walked back toward Eastern Standard.

People on their way to look at the dead man were streaming towards us the whole way down. When we got to Second Street, we turned around and looked back. We could see the flashing cop lights up the mall where Kai lay. It still didn't feel real.

Mick and I shook hands goodbye in front of the Standard. I stood before the big glass window staring in. I had been thinking about Sam the whole way down. I wished I could tell her about Kai. Like Sam, like Susan, he had wanted in some intangible way to help me.

162

I thought about all the men and women that had filtered through my classrooms. Kai had been one of the really smart ones who had the trendy new lingo down pat. But at the end of his life there was no jargon in what he said. Trust me. "Rightsized" is not a post modern ideal. Closing my eyes, I could see the look on his face as he offered to tell me his story. Unlike most of the faces I had seen this night, that look had nothing to do with testosterone or pheromones or drugs or bourbon. Most of what I heard in that room tonight were fragments of stories told by men who were non-starters in the world of the sainted dollar.

I opened my eyes upon Susan and Eden lost in talk, seated at a table along the sidewall, laughing, happy. I could not hear a thing, thank God, but it was good to see them so. Then a woman at a table against the window looked up at me and blanched. In a momentary reflection caused by the street light behind me as I recoiled — I caught sight of what she had seen — my face beaten and swollen and even to me unrecognizable. I had no wish to share it. Certainly not with Susan and Eden.

I moved on. As I turned the corner, I saw the big white Continental, the biggest thing in a parking lot filled with Teutonic and Nordic Euro Tech — Beamers, Jettas, Mercedes', Saabs — it seemed almost to beckon me to the long journey south. In the glove box was my escape kit: a passport, maps, money, cigarettes, and in the back seat, enough unopened mail to cure anyone's insomnia.

I got in. I sat behind the wheel for what felt like a very long time. I felt like hell. My face throbbed like one big toothache. As I sat there I suddenly had an image in my mind of my father, of what he had looked like as he sat where I sat now, of his frozen impassive expression. It was like the Scotch he drank. The one that never varies. I don't like Scotch and I used to think he bought it for the motto as much as for the taste.

Without realizing it, I was reaching down for my last-ditch pint of bourbon which was not there and was not there. Then I remembered what it had looked like where I had last seen it, standing beside the curb in front of Susan's house two nights ago. Then my thoughts dissolved into a brownout.

Turn on the key, I thought. I turned it, and instantly the motor started. Craning my neck in agony, I backed out and pulled up to High Street.

I sat there a while trying to collect myself.

If I turned left I'd be heading south. In a week or so I'd be back where I started from, where Katie had put me out on the Pan American Highway three months ago at the overlook to Lake Atitlán. I buried my face between my hands where they gripped the steering wheel. As I sat there, I had the strongest sensation that Sam was sitting beside me. It seemed to me that I could actually hear her breathing, deep and soft and even.

But even before I opened my eyes, I knew she'd slipped away. Not from what I call my heart. She'd be there waiting for me in one of those moments I'd spent the last four months drinking to keep from remembering. Good old memory, always there when you wanted it least.

Then I remembered, though I'd never really ceased to think of him, the man I'd left back there, lying on his back on the mall. For I owed him. Thanks to me, he would never tell his story again.

I knew something about the end of it that needed telling. And who else to tell it if not me? If I turned right, I'd be making a decision to tell it, how he came to lie where I'd last seen him. I owed him that at least.

Still I sat there. It bothered me that it would be my story I'd be telling as much as his. The so-called teacher, a self-indulgent refugee from life, if you could call what I'd been living a life.

No post mortems, I thought.

"Go left," I heard myself say.

Again, I sat there, decided but unmoving. My head was throbbing. I felt like I was blacking out. Suddenly behind me a pair of lights on high beam exploded. A horn blared. And without thinking I turned the wheel. I turned right. It was like the car had made the decision. As I drove very slowly up High Street, past Fellini's, past the flashing lights of the police cars where Kai lay, past the extinguished lights of the Acid House, I tried to picture myself stumbling through the doors of the police station. I turned down that street. I saw two policemen smoking outside, one a tall, raw-boned, red-faced man, with stiff looking yellow hair, the other a big black man in dark oversized glasses.

I pushed the power window button. Slowly the driver window glided down.

The black cop, his eyes wary under the shaded lenses, dropped his butt and walked over to my car.

"Something happen to you tonight, sir?"

Well, last time I'd seen my face it looked like Brando's at the end of *On the Waterfront*. I nodded. I kept nodding. I was trying to talk.

"That boy — man — who died tonight on the mall," I said finally.

"Yeah?"

"I was who they wanted."

"Who is they?"

The other cop standing beside him had asked that. I could tell they both thought I was drunk. And I couldn't blame them. It was taking me a lot of time to get the words out.

164

"Kin," I said finally.

"You been drinking, Chief?" said the white cop.

I shook my head. I was afraid again that I was starting to black out. The pain was getting worse too.

"You say the people who killed the victim were your kin."

I nodded. I was starting to sweat.

"It's going to take a while for me to tell the story," I said. My voice was failing. The black cop opened the door and put his hand on my shoulder.

"Let me help you out, sir. You don't look real good."

When he said that, it was like my mind got traction for just a second. "I ain't good," I said, "but I'm a better version of me than I've been for longer than I remember."

The white cop took hold of my arm. His eyes said that he had heard it all before.

"Whatever you say, Chief. Whatever you say."